MW01043406

PAX ROMANA II

ESCAPE FROM BABYLON

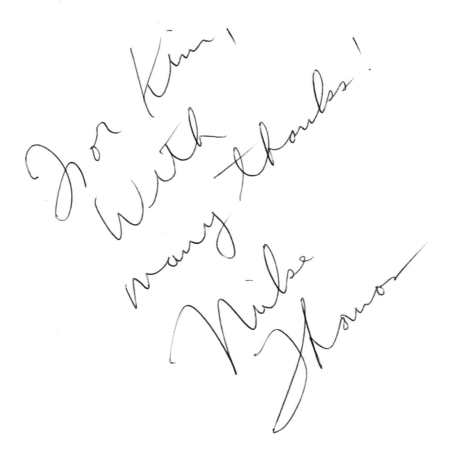

For Kim,
With
many thanks!
Mike Thomas

Michael Thomas

"All that is fleeting is only a simile."
Johann Wolfgang von Goethe,
Faust, Chorus Mysticus, Part II

"And certainly the glass *was* beginning to melt away,
just like a bright, silvery mist."
Lewis Carroll, *Through the Looking Glass*

"And the dragon and his angels fought back."
Revelation 12:7

PART I

—1—

ASIAN ANGEL

O Rome, in your greatness, in your beauty,
That which was secure has fled,
and only that which is fleeting remains and lasts.
Francisco de Quevedo (1580-1645)

Mark is ready to fire and take out Seren when he suddenly hears a voice cry out.

"Mark, behind you!!!"

Almost without thinking, he drops his rifle, flips over on his back, and withdraws his sidearm. As he does, he sees a large drone hovering over him. It discharges a flash plasma burst, and he moves to dodge it, but the burst grazes his right arm. He manages to return fire and destroys the drone.

Though still in pain and bleeding, Mark leaps to his feet and jumps on his aerobike. He quickly starts it and takes off. He assumes that whoever was guiding the drone will not be far behind him, and he is right.

Mark glances back and, after spotting his pursuer, he plummets straight down toward the pavement below. He then pulls up abruptly and enters into a series of erratic turns, darting in and out of large cracks in buildings split open by the earthquakes.

Mark calculates that his pursuer is operating a bike much faster than his, so he has to rely on cunning and on being more random. He leans hard to the right or to the left as he makes sharp turns. He dives and ascends abruptly and then disappears into half-fallen buildings, emerging on the other side.

Despite his evasive maneuvers, his pursuer mirrors him successfully and is soon joined by another aerobike, and then still another. They seem to be multiplying and closing in. All three are blasting at will. Mark tries to return fire, but it's nearly impossible for him to aim at these speeds. He has to concentrate on zigzagging, as he knows that it's only a matter of time before they hit him since his bike has no weapons or shielding.

As soon as Mark thinks he is losing them again, a message appears on the display of his oracle glasses:

"PG DEACTIVATION IN 5 SECONDS."

"Oh, shit!" Mark is about to lose his operations belt, his glasses, everything hi-tech.

The counter finally hits *0.* His belt goes dark, and his glasses go blank.

When Mark and the aerobike begin to fall, he remembers that he commandeered it with his Praetorian Guard credentials. All his instruments have gone dark as well.

As he descends and sees the ground rapidly approaching, Mark remembers that the voice he had heard, the one that warned him of the imminent attack from the drone, was Dominique's.

He thinks, "*Chérie, if you're in heaven now, I'll see you soon!*"

But suddenly someone or something latches onto his collar and pulls him up.

"I've got you, Captain Knutson!!!" The pilot has leaned over and tilted the bike to grab him.

Funny, it doesn't sound like Mikhail.

Mark briefly watches his aerobike drop beneath him and crash and then grabs upward for something to hang on to. He sees another aerobike and its pilot, who is wearing an odd helmet, and he struggles to climb up on it. The pursuers are still firing flash bursts, but their blasts are deflected by his rescuer's fully operational energy shield.

Once Mark is locked securely on board, the aerobike accelerates to a blinding speed and leaves the pursuers far behind, at least for the moment.

I didn't know an aerobike could move this fast.

As far as Mark can tell, the pilot does a complete circle around Rome in a matter of seconds. His rescuer then comes up behind the pursuers and opens fire on them.

None of the hostiles is hit, but they all veer off and lose themselves among the wreckage of toppled buildings. The mysterious pilot then accelerates yet again at what seems like light speed and heads straight for the Circus Maximus, which has been severely damaged and is completely empty.

The pilot sets the bike down gently on vertical blue flames and a soft cushion created by the release of pressurized air. They both sit motionless for just a moment as the engine winds down.

Mark breathes a sigh of relief and steps off the bike, wanting to thank his rescuer.

The pilot also steps off and removes a pink helmet; her thick, black hair flows out as she takes it off. Much to Mark's surprise, she is a diminutive Asian wearing tall boots and a long military-style jacket. Her almost black hair is just short of shoulder-length and carefully groomed.

"Uh, thank you...uh..."

"My name is Mei-Li, that's Chinese for 'beautiful,' in case you were wondering."

She shakes his hand and adds, "Tien-Shi Mei-Li. To you that would mean 'beautiful ambassador from Heaven.'"

"Thank you very much, May Lee Ten Shoot, you are definitely heaven-sent!"

"You can thank your friend, Mikhail, as well. He sent me to see if you needed any help."

Mei-Li speaks strongly, boldly, with a certain authority.

She's a shrimp, Mark thinks, still surprised. *She doesn't look strong enough to have caught me and pulled me up onto the bike.*

"So are you also with Search and Rescue?" he asks with a tone of disbelief.

"I know that I'm small in your eyes," she retorts, as if able to read his thoughts, "but as you Americans say, I pack a punch. Your arm looks bad. I have something for that."

As Mark carefully pulls back the burnt part of his sleeve, she withdraws a small cloth from a utility pack and presses it onto his wound.

"I really am grateful, but I do have a question. Why did you bring me here to the Circus Maximus?"

"We need to be in a wide-open space, a place where we can see them coming."

"Them?"

"Yes, I think they're just about here. Do you hear them?"

Mark listens carefully and notices an intense buzzing; it sounds like a swarm of insects. He looks up at the sky and sees a large black cloud that is obscuring the sun and is descending on the Circus like a storm at sea, like a Rogue Storm. Mark had scarcely begun enjoying seeing the sun again, but now the entire Circus is being covered by a murky, restless shell, an inky blackness challenged only by the lights on Mei-Li's aerobike.

"What is that cloud? I've never seen anything like that before. Is it a storm?"

"Something you'll be seeing a lot more of in the near future. You're being allowed to see it just for now."

"It doesn't look good. In fact, it looks evil. Are we equipped to fight it? I only have my one gun with metal bullets."

"We're equipped," answers Mei-Li nonchalantly. She opens her long jacket and withdraws two swords that appear to catch fire as quickly as she pulls them out.

They remind Mark of the sword he used to slay the Emerald-Green Dragon in *Sleeping Beauty*. They have gleaming gold handles with inset red jewels, and their blades give off a blazing light that is almost blinding.

The appearance of the swords seems to cause a stir above. The gloomy cloud becomes wildly agitated.

"They sound like locusts. Is that what they are?"

"Sort of."

Mei-Li does not seem rattled. She extends both swords high above her head and then crosses them, causing them to touch each other. When they do, they discharge a torrent of brilliant light. In fact, Mark has to cover his eyes for several seconds.

When he opens them again, he sees sunlight again. The insect cloud has vanished.

"How did you do that? Where did you get those swords? Is this a hologame?"

"Patience, captain. All your questions will be answered in time. I have a message from Mikhail. He respectfully requests that you return to your apartment and stay there. He will visit you in a few days with more information and instructions."

"What's going on?"

"It's important that you do as he asks. There's a plan in motion, and you're an important part of it. Those locusts seemed to have taken a great interest in you."

"What? What plan? Locusts interested in me? Lady, either you're insane or I am. Hey, the whole world has just gone to hell! How can I go back to my apartment and act like everything is normal?"

"Go and stay there! He'll be coming to see you, along with your friend, Iqhawe."

"Really!"

"Yes, and I will come, too."

"Really!"

"I think he has a new type of hologame that he wants to play with you."

"Really! You *are* all insane. I mean, I love hologames, but is this the time?"

"You'll understand when you get into it."

The aerobikes that were previously pursuing them have tracked their present location and enter the airspace of the Circus. Mark estimates that there are at least a dozen or more of them. They all land in a wide circle around Mark and Mei-Li.

Mei-Li comments, "They think they have found their prey. Take my bike and return to your apartment."

"Uh, I think our friends here might have an objection to that."

"Oh, don't worry about them," she says as the recent arrivals dismount their bikes, raise their weapons, and close in.

Mei-Li thinks for a moment. "Let's see...temporary blindness should do the trick."

She spins her swords in circles producing a sort of starburst, after which all the shadowy figures stumble and fall flat on their faces. They are completely disoriented and helpless.

"I've also deactivated their weapons and various tech systems."

"How?" Mark is amazed.

"Don't worry about how I did it. Take my bike and get yourself home."

"And how will you get home?" *Wherever that is.*

"I'll be fine. Just get on your way. I'll stay and deal with these hoodlums."

"I guess you know what you're doing."

"I do. Don't worry."

"Those swords. They look familiar."

"You used one before, I know."

"Yeah, but in a hologame."

"This is not a hologame. Mikhail will explain everything to you when we visit. Be on your way now."

Mark salutes Mei-Li in a flippant way, and then he mounts the bike and blasts off. It looks like a regular aerobike, except that it's pink. As he sets a course to his apartment, he studies the instruments. Everything looks standard. He can't figure out how to run it up to that astounding speed that Mei-Li had achieved.

As he gains altitude, Mark again views the devastation of a once elegant and technologically advanced city. Rome now in ruins. His life in ruins. A life that will never return. He wonders how long it will take to rebuild the city. It seems an almost impossible task.

Soon, Mark is aware that he has company. Two aerobikes have achieved a parallel course, and their riders are looking him over with some interest.

"*Cosa è questo?*" one rider calls out to the other. Mark judges they are not PGs, but thugs. They seem to be laughing at him, that he is riding a pink aerobike.

He thinks he knows what their next move is, but before he can do anything, Mei-Li's voice comes over the i-com. It's as if she somehow knows he has run into trouble.

"Captain, I forgot to mention something. If you require more velocity, be sure you are locked in, and just hit that pink button on the control panel in front of you. It should be flashing now. And hold on tight!"

Even as the two original bikers are joined by three more, Mark hits the indicated button, and he streaks away from the group. He's not used to this speed on a bike, so he pulls up quickly, trying to avoid hitting a megabuilding directly in his path.

Mark finally slows the bike down and regains control.

Wow, he thinks, *I gotta get me one of these! Just not in pink....*

—2—

DREAM OF THE RED CHAMBER

"Truth becomes fiction whenever the fiction is true;
And real becomes unreal when the unreal is real."
— Cao Xueqin, *The Story of the Stone*

Mark sets a course back to his apartment building and heads toward a public balcony opening at the end of the hall on his floor. He dismounts the bike and tries to figure out how to secure it, but it takes off by itself and seems to follow some pre-programmed course.

Now I'm completely without transportation and have no Praetorian Guard operations belt or oracle glasses, Mark thinks as he watches the bike fly away.

As he enters the building through the balcony, he sees that it is completely dark. He uses the light from his portapack, and when he reaches his door, he extracts a key from the pack. *Time warp. I haven't had to use a key since I was a kid.*

He opens the door and enters. As he suspected, everything is dark, completely without power.

He looks around. His control panel shows that there is a small amount of battery power left, but he decides not to use it. Pinocchio is still shut down. The robot stands there like a silent guard over a dark, empty domain. Pinocchio may have some reserve power, but Mark will not activate him for the time being.

Mark calculates that he can use his portapack at minimum power for quite a while and that he can tie it into his system. After quickly consuming a melted protein bar and a warm energy drink, Mark lies down on his sofa, pushing it toward his entertainment center. He is beginning to struggle with a depression that he knew would come.

He turns on the projector via his portapack and scrolls through his files. He projects small 3-D images of Dominique onto the floor across from him. In order to conserve power, he keeps all the images at a low resolution and about one-half meter high.

There she stands, like an exquisite porcelain doll. Mark feels better just looking at her image, but he also brushes away a tear. Every image triggers a memory. She doesn't have to move or speak or dance to keep him interested.

He remembers the music boxes his mother used to have in her bedroom. She must have had a dozen or more. At times he would go into her room and wind them all up. All the minute ballerinas would then dance and turn to the beat of a numerous competing and dissonant tunes.

Mark then scrolls through his music. He finally decides to listen to all nine symphonies of Beethoven, beginning with the first. At least for now, he can leave behind a wrecked world and focus on the sublime beauty of a petite figurine who is unknowingly being accompanied by a symphony orchestra.

"Rotate figurine."

At this command, Dominique's hologram turns slowly and gracefully like one of those small, porcelain ballerinas in her mother's bedroom. She's smiling.

During the second symphony, he switches to a rotating slide show of Dominique holograms. As he gazes on the small figures, it occurs to him that he needs to return to her apartment to retrieve anything he can, especially some of her books and as much of her hololibrary as possible.

Mark lies there in the shadows thinking and remembering, as Dominique's images pass in review. First she is dancing, then playing the piano, then cooking, then standing in front of the Eiffel Tower, always radiant, her eyes vibrant with love for him.

He decides to switch the presentation from "shuffle" to "chronological."

There she is once again, sitting at her desk at EuroSecure, making that Orange Alert announcement. Once again, he watches the "Birth of Venus." Then, the program passes to the artificially manufactured image of her facing him in the boat.

Mark skips the image of her sitting across from him in the hypertrain studiously trying to ignore him. He then accesses the day in the *Parco Centrale* when she really was sitting across from him, as they were listening to Swan Lake.

After enjoying that experience again, he goes carefully and slowly through the dinner and dating sequences, leading to the first kiss. The Paris file is rich, right up to the proposal at L'Opéra. Mark strains to re-live it all via technology supplemented by his memory, but it's not the same. It's over. It was like a dream.

His life will never be the same. She's gone. This is not *The Nutcracker*, in which they are magically transported to the Land of Sweets to live happily ever after. It's not a fairy tale like *Sleeping Beauty*. Still it was a little like a fairy tale in some ways. He did save her life in the real world, but they were together for such a short time. It all happened so fast. There wasn't even time enough for them to have a disagreement or a fight.

So little time together, and it ended so quickly.

Mark feels himself breaking inside. He thinks about reading the French Bible in her apartment, about those verses and about that prayer that gave him peace.

Why?

That peace is still with him, even though a cloud of depression is hovering over him like the locusts at the Circus.

Why?

He doesn't understand anything. Dominique is gone, and it's likely he will never see her again. Why?

Sometime during Beethoven's 5th, Mark falls asleep.

He finds himself in Dominique's house in Paris, in the entryway. He calls out to her or to anyone who might be there.

No one answers.

He looks for the staircase, but he can't find it. He sees the paintings hanging on the walls and walks over to his favorite, the little girl swimming with the swans.

As he stares into the picture, it comes alive. Dominique is moving, but she's not a little girl; she's a young woman. She's smiling and laughing. And the swans have been transformed into women in white. She seems so happy as she gracefully swims toward the shore.

Mark looks at the bank and sees her father and mother waiting for her at the water's edge. Even though he can recognize them both, they seem so strangely young. Her father extends his hand and helps her out of the water.

The scene fades, as does the house.

Now Mark is in a dark room with a brightly lit window, which he approaches. It's about the size of the painting. He peers in and sees Dominique! She looks exquisitely beautiful as she comes up to the glass and sits down. She's looking into it, straight at Mark, but she's acting like she's in front of a mirror, brushing her hair.

Dominique is wearing a long white dress that somehow looks like a wedding dress. But no, that's not possible.

Mark yells at the top of his lungs and waves his hands, "*Chérie*! It's me! Are we getting married?"

She doesn't appear to see or hear him. Behind her are other women, the same women he saw swimming with her. They are gathered all around her, attending to her every need.

The room is small, covered with ornate red wallpaper and what seem like thousands of red roses. It's like a classical painting with Dominique as the centerpiece. She's smiling large. She has never looked so beautiful or quite so thrilled.

Her female attendants place a tiara on her head. Mark remembers the one she wore at L'Opéra in Paris for the *Nutcracker*. But no, this one has many more fiery jewels.

The maids also place other jewelry on her wrists and even a jeweled belt around her waist. They then put a large necklace around her neck. It is a gold chain attached to a thin gold plate that is covered with twelve different stones of various colors.

Mark easily recognizes an emerald and what might be a sapphire. The others are all precious stones, but he is not completely sure what they are. Dominique stands and turns to the right and then to the left, still looking at herself in the glass.

Suddenly Mark hears a loud buzzing sound behind him. He drops to the floor and rolls over. As he suspected, it's the locusts, and they're coming in force and fast.

With no seeming interest in him, they crash into the window, but the window remains intact. The evil, dark cloud repeatedly attacks the transparent pane with no effect. None of the hideous creatures seems to notice him. He stands to his feet, reaching for a sidearm.

Mark looks down and notices he is wearing two swords. They have ornate gold handles with inset rubies, just like the sword in the hologame that he used to slay the dragon and like the swords that Mei-Li had brandished.

He decides to withdraw them. As he does, they light up the dark room, radiating a brilliant power. He thinks about how Mei-Li had used them. When he crosses them over his head, they likewise emit a burst of light, which quickly disperses the demonic cloud of insects.

Yet he still senses an evil presence. Out of the darkness emerges a figure that initially looks like a huge locust. As it approaches him, he sees that there is something serpentine about the way it moves as it comes near Mark. *A hybrid?*

Mark stands between this unidentified thing and the window. He raises both swords and is poised to do battle if necessary. The insect moves in even closer, and Mark sees that it has a tail like a scorpion, complete with a stinger. Mark remembers his first challenger in the desert when he was beginning to play *Sleeping Beauty – Infinity Version.*

He taunts it, "So, if it isn't another monster bug come to its exterminator!"

The creature suddenly extends its wings, which begin flapping and whirring at high speed, creating a deafening sound. Its mouth has large teeth, and it has begun roaring like a lion.

Mark stands his ground. He thinks, "*This guy looks like he could bust through that window…. Over my dead body.*"

As Mark moves toward the demonic insect, it occurs to him that he is probably dreaming. If that is true, this thing can't hurt him or Dominique; nothing in this realm can.

He runs toward his opponent with great gusto, raising his right sword in the air as he attacks. A second before he brings the sword down, he notices something large approaching from his left.

It's another large locust, but he has no time to switch course. He buries his sword into the first insect's head, slicing sharply downward. One down and dead, but he won't have time to withdraw that sword. He quickly tries to extend the sword in his left hand.

Out of nowhere a figure appears between him and the second charging monster bug. It looks like Mei-Li. She stands in the gap and wields both her swords, decapitating the beast in his tracks. After it falls in front of her, she turns around, staring at Mark.

"Good job!" Mark jokes, "I saw a move like that in a bullfight once." Then he laughs, but Mei-Li does not.

"This is not a game, captain," she rebukes him somberly. "You could have been killed."

"Look, I just realized that I'm dreaming all this."

"It's not a dream either," Mei-Li retorts. "Wake up!"

Mark opens his eyes, startled. He looks around at his apartment and feels a shiver run up his spine.

"Okay, I'm awake!" Mark blurts out. He's getting tired of everyone telling him to wake up. He looks around the room again trying to get his bearings and to be sure he's not dreaming again.

He only sees Pinocchio, and the robot's not saying a thing. The system is still playing Beethoven's 5th. No time seems to have passed.

Mark resumes his slide show.

—3—

DAWN'S PALE FINGERS

Eventually Mark falls asleep again and is awakened at about 5:00 a. m. by the power coming on in his apartment. He jumps up from his couch and spins in a circle with his hand on his sidearm. The lights are all on, and even Pinocchio comes out of his self-induced trance.

"Geppetto! May I wake up now?"

"Activate, Pinocchio. I guess I will need you again. Do a diagnostic on all systems."

"All systems fully functional, Father. Would you like something to eat or drink?'

Mark sits back down without replying. He has to get his head together and figure out what is going on.

"Can we access external cameras?"

At this, Pinocchio ties into the system and the entertainment section becomes a window on the world.

"All four walls, all directions."

Pinocchio complies.

Mark turns again in a circle to behold Rome at night. There are lights everywhere but no holograms or ads.

"Increase brightness and contrast so I can see in the dark."

As Pinocchio makes the adjustment, Mark notices small armies of megabots active on virtually every street he can see.

These giant, five-to-ten story robots were previously banned from Rome itself and used only in the mines, the factories, and the fields, and for possible defense against attack. They are tireless, efficient, and follow orders without question. Currently they are clearing the rubble and removing larger fragments of fallen buildings. Smaller machines are removing dead bodies, which are strewn everywhere.

They didn't waste any time, Mark thinks.

"Pinocchio, do we have access to any news channels?"

"Yes, Father, but you have one message pending that is required before we can be given access."

"Required?" Mark can only wonder.

"Okay, play it in 2-D." Pinocchio complies, but the program suddenly seems taken over by a holographic transmission.

Standing before him is Senator Romanus Santori.

Mark remembers, *The fiery orator.* "Let's see what he has to say. English."

When the virtual statue comes to life and starts talking, Mark realizes that he has control only over which language he is hearing. The hologram is being remotely controlled.

"Friends, Romans, countrymen, listen to me! Many of you may not know me. I am Romanus Santori, formerly a member of the Roman Senate. Our great city has suffered loss, but I bring good news. You may have seen the megabots working diligently to clear the streets of rubble."

The hologram now includes scenes from the streets.

"Soon, the robots will begin rebuilding. For a time, it appeared that 'The Sweet Life,' the Roman dream, and the Roman peace, were lost! Now we now have hope of a better tomorrow. I realize this may seem unbelievable to some of you, but look outside your buildings if you have not; they are working around the clock. There is no more Haze. And our Lord Seren is solely responsible. If you do not know him, you soon will. He has been our rock and steadfast leader in this tragedy, this great crisis."

Santori turns and extends his left hand, as if to welcome someone. In short order, a life-sized hologram of a smiling Seren joins him in the room.

Mark remembers Santori's speech in the senate. He's still an impressive speaker, but his tone and message have changed radically. It's like he's helping to pave the way for the new Caesar.

He goes on, "Hundreds of thousands have died in the recent earthquakes and collateral damage, among these, our beloved Roman Senate and scores of leaders at all levels. We officials who remain have elected Seren as temporary overseer of the rebuilding of Rome. We have given him authority because this extraordinary man has power, real power, the power to heal, the power to transform, and the power to multiply our food supply. I have seen him at work, and I can assure you that it is real!"

Mark again muses at the irony, *And this is the guy who was railing against Caesars.* Then Mark remembers Massi and what some people do when the wind changes.

Santori continues, "Be aware that we have reorganized the Praetorian Guard for a time of transition. Once previous guard members have been approved, they will continue in their service. In addition, we have a new elite security force which we have chosen to call 'The Sentinels.' Most all are former guard members. Each group wears distinctive uniforms. Remember that they are here to protect you and to defend Rome from her enemies."

Santori seems to conjure up another figure, a woman. He points to her gray uniform with a scarlet stripe down the sides of the pants and scarlet highlights on her jacket.

"This is the new Praetorian Guard uniform and will help you to identify them."

He produces another figure who is wearing a uniform with a scarlet cape. The coat and pants are also scarlet with a black stripe down the pant legs and black highlights.

"And this is an example of the Sentinel's uniform."

Mark studies the two, looking for weapons, but these, at least their holograms, seem to be unarmed. He'll need to have a closer look when he sees some real examples.

Santori continues his explanation of the new order. "You will also be seeing Seren's disciples, who wear scarlet robes. They have learned how to harness just a little of his power. You will see them heal the sick and injured and feed Rome and bring wealth and prosperity to the Eternal City on a scale never before imagined, much greater than anything we have thus far experienced. We are on the verge of a new Renaissance, a new beginning for Rome and for humanity!"

All this rhetoric sounds familiar.

He remembers Angela's last words of warning about Seren and his "disciples."

"Pinocchio, end message."

The senator disappears but the hologram of Seren remains in the room, which Mark finds a little unsettling.

"Pinocchio, did you end the message and delete?"

"Yes, Father."

"Then, what is that?" Mark says, pointing to Seren.

"I am not sure, Father. There still seems to be an override in the system."

Mark walks over to the virtual statue, which is smiling and waving, and puts his hand through it. He then moves around behind it and then walks in front of it.

"Pinocchio, is it possible that this image can see us? Or that through this holographic presence, someone could be watching us?"

"I do not know, Geppetto. The holofile name is 'Seren is watching over you.'"

"*Great,*" Mark thinks. "*Now I feel better.*"

He goes and sits on the couch. He considers pulling out his sidearm and firing a bullet into the image, *but that would just waste a bullet and put a hole in the wall.* He decides to sit for a while and try to ignore his unwelcomed visitor.

After about an hour, Seren disappears.

Mark decides to see what is going on in the rest of the world.

"Pinocchio, access the news. Display."

Six icons appear, floating in mid-air. "Entertainment" and "Weather" are marked "unavailable."

"World news," Mark commands with a certain sense of dread.

Images of destruction file across Mark's apartment while a somewhat grim narrator gives details.

"Recovery from earthquakes and tsunamis has been slow around the globe. We have no way of knowing how many people have died. Some estimates are over one billion. All the world's major tectonic plates have shifted, including the Pacific and Antarctic plates, which triggered cataclysmic tidal waves. Movements in the Eurasian and Indian plates caused massive quakes and have brought life in those areas to a standstill. There is grave concern about possible famines, epidemics, and anarchy as governments struggle to restore order."

"News from the Federation."

A conference of Federation leaders appears. They seem to be involved in an intense discussion.

"In the Federation, damage was irregular. Most cities suffered catastrophic damage while others experienced only a little. Rome was hardest hit, but scattered reports claim that clean-up efforts are already underway. The Federation, acknowledging recent actions by the surviving Roman senate, has recognized Seren as Overseer of Rome and the Italian peninsula."

Mark notices that one icon is marked "The Haze," and he selects it.

"Scientists from around the world are in fierce debate about the cause for the widespread earthquakes. Some have suggested a relationship between the quakes, tsunamis, and the mysterious disappearance of the Haze, although others call it simply a freak occurrence of nature. In Rome, claims abound that Seren is responsible. Such claims, of course, have been dismissed by the world scientific community; they note that the Haze has merely re-gathered in large regions of the Pacific and the southern hemisphere."

After watching the news updates, Mark decides to go back to listening to music and to watching holograms of Dominique. He lies on the couch and relaxes for several hours.

At about 8:30 a. m., Pinocchio informs him that he has an incoming call.

"Who is it?"

"Identified as Massimo Sansone."

Mark approves and in no time, Massi's hologram is standing in his living room.

"Knutson! You're still alive? You son-of-a-bitch! But I have to say that I'm glad to see you."

"Hey, Massi."

Massi squints his eyes and stares at Mark.

"What's wrong? You are still glad to see me?"

"Man! I thought the image was bad or something. You haven't shaved for a while?"

"I don't remember the last time."

"You know, with a beard, you look a lot like Seren!"

Mark rolls his eyes.

"Yeah? So I'm told."

"Anyway, I wondered if I could come over and talk for a while. I have a proposal for you."

"A proposal?"

"Yeah, let me come and explain."

In an hour or so, Massi is at the door. He comes in and smacks Mark on the arm.

"*Ciao*, you asshole. I knew you'd make it! But hey, you look even more like Seren in person. Ha! You'd better shave or some people will start worshiping you."

"I don't think so. Come in and have a seat. Do you want something to eat? A beer maybe?"

Mark notices that Massi is wearing a new uniform that identifies him as a PG in the new order of things.

"Sure, a beer is always good."

Pinocchio serves him, and he sits down on the couch and takes a long drink.

"So what's with the new uniform?"

"It's a uniform I hope you'll be wearing soon, *amico*."

"Same operations belt and standard gear?"

"The same."

Mark explains, "I still have my belt, but it was deactivated recently. They apparently didn't waste any time."

"Look, remember what I told you last time I saw you, hovering over Rome during the quakes? I said that Seren was next. He's the man with the power, and you'd best align yourself with him. That's what I told you. Some PGs were on board long before the quakes. Others came later. If you sign up now, it will still be easy. You'll be a Sentinel in no time!"

"Massi, I'm not sure I agree with all this—"

"Agreement has nothing to do with anything, at least not for me. Wake up, Knutson. This is about power in a new reality. But you know, it's not all bad. Think of it. Everything is better. Everyone benefits. And if you play your cards right, you end up high on the food chain. Hey, I know it may be hard to swallow initially. I know they cut you off quick, but don't take it personally. They just started over; they did it with everybody. It makes sense."

"I figured. I just caught a newscast in which Santori explained it all. You've done that apparently? So what, do you hope to become a Sentinel?"

"That's what I'm anticipating. For now, I'm okay just being a part of the transitional Praetorian Guard. If I do good work, I'll have a good shot at the more elite group. Come on, Knutson! It's a new world! I hope you'll consider becoming a part. Like I told you, man, Seren needs guys like you. With your experience... Hey, *amico*, remember your old buddy when you become a general!"

Massi laughs loudly. "I already put in a good word for you, like I promised. The rest is up to you."

"Look, Massi, I appreciate your confidence, but a lot has happened. I'm having a hard time dealing with it."

"Hey, did you ever find your fiancée? What was her name?"

"Dominique. She was French. I never located her. I can only assume..."

"I'm sorry, man, I really am. I guess you and Angela never got back together?"

"Angela is dead."

Massi looks stunned, but just for a moment.

"*Amico*, I'm so sorry! I didn't know. A lot of people have died. It's been bad."

Mark does not mention how Angela died or his theory about Seren's involvement.

23

"Anyway, let's focus on the now. The destruction is in the past. Have you heard what Seren is doing to rebuild?"

"Yeah, I watched the news and I looked out. A lot of megabots have been called in apparently. It almost looks like this was planned well in advance."

"Yeah, I never realized there were so many robots in Italy. It's almost like Seren is having the old ones build new ones. You would think it was an army or something. Make no mistake, Seren is in the know and has been planning all this for a long time. But like I said, it's all good stuff, and this is just the beginning. We have real hope, *amico*. You just have to catch the vision. This is going to be big. This is going to change the whole world and everything we've previously known."

Mark remembers similar words coming from Angela. Then he asks, "Massi, did Seren plan the earthquakes? Or maybe even cause them somehow?"

Massi looks puzzled for a moment. "He does have power, but why would he use it that way? It doesn't make any sense."

"No, it doesn't."

"Look, Knutson, I get you. You're a good guy, a warrior with honor. I admire and respect you. Think of it this way. You can be a part of all the good that's coming. You can make a difference. Now you have the chance to get in on the ground floor. Now is the time to act."

"Thanks, Massi, I'll consider it. I'm going to try to check in at EuroSecure headquarters in Naples. I've had no communication with them, but even when I do, I'm not sure what I'll find there."

They chat for a while longer. After Massi leaves, Mark runs into the bathroom and shaves.

Within only a few minutes, Pinocchio announces another incoming call.

"It's Mikhail."

—4—

THE UPWARD JOURNEY

"Your time will come. You will face the same Evil,
and you will defeat it." – Arwen, *Lord of the Rings*

Mikhail asks if he can come over and bring Iqhawe and Mei-Li. When they arrive, Mark is glad to see them. Mikhail is jovial, as always. Iqhawe and Mei-Li are serious, as always.

Mikhail gives him a hug, Iqhawe shakes his hand and smiles faintly, and Mei-Li just stares at him. They are an odd-looking group, a sort of strange mismatch: a large, jovial Russian; a larger, solemn African; and a petite Asian woman who "packs a punch." He notices that Iqhawe is carrying a rather large case.

"Captain! We are so happy to see you."

"Likewise, Mikhail, and you can drop the 'captain' title. I'm not an officer or soldier in anything as far as I know. I guess I'm dreading checking in with EuroSecure."

"Communications are down for now. We haven't been able to contact anyone either. I think it may be more of a security issue rather than a technical one. Today, we're here to enlist you as a warrior in another cause. A greater one."

Pinocchio creates spontaneous seating for the three visitors.

"You have met Mei-Li, I believe?"

"Yes! Mei-Li. And I think I remember your last name, 'Teen Sure' or was it 'Ten Four?'" Mark laughs awkwardly.

"Tien-Shi," Mei-Li corrects him without seeming to be in on the joke.

"I haven't seen Mei-Li since...since..." Mark looks at her meaningfully.

She responds, "Since the Circus Maximus?"

"Since you beheaded that huge locust in the dark room."

Mei-Li shrugs, "You must have dreamt that one."

Mikhail continues, "With your permission, captain, we don't feel comfortable calling you anything else. You are always an honored warrior to us." Iqhawe nods his head in agreement.

"Thanks, but I have a question."

Mark hesitates a moment as he surveys the motley crew standing before him.

"Who are you people anyway? Are you really with Search and Rescue?"

Mikhail laughs, "Of course, captain! I believe that each one of us has saved you at one time or another. I would say that we are really quite good at what we do."

Mark leans back in his chair. "No argument there."

"We are committed to saving lives, but we do have another job, in fact, a sort of mission, one that we want you to be a part of."

"That's what I wanted to ask about. Mei-Li said something about it before. What's that about?"

"You are aware of what is happening in Rome?"

"I just watched some newscasts and reports when the power came back on."

"What you have seen is only the beginning. Seren has risen to power, and his influence will spread quickly."

"Seren is evil," Iqhawe interjects.

Mark responds immediately, "I know."

"Our mission is a two-fold one. First, we will continue our search and rescue efforts, except that we will also be covertly evacuating those who desire to leave Rome quietly and leave no tracks."

Mark asks, "Why do we need to evacuate them from Rome? Can't they just leave?"

Mikhail responds: "That is easy for you, captain. You have official standing. But we know that even now, many people are disappearing, and we know why. The need for safe passage will increase as more people become disillusioned with Seren and begin asking questions, as did Angela. Such people either disappear or die."

"Okay, I get it."

"Eventually, Seren will enslave the naïve and slaughter the innocent, and, make no mistake, he will persecute believers."

"Believers?"

"Yes, captain. You have become one, have you not?"

Mark thinks about reading Dominique's Bible in her apartment.

"Dominique was a believer."

"Yes, she was."

"Then I am a believer, too. I came to peace in her apartment while reading some Bible verses that she had underlined."

All three visitors smile, but Mark tears up.

"She's dead, isn't she?"

"No, captain, she's now more alive than ever. She has passed on to the City. But you will get a chance to see her, yes, even today."

Mark is in disbelief. "I'm dying today?"

"No, captain," Mikhail laughs gently. "The second part of our mission is to prepare you for a confrontation with Seren."

"Bring it on."

"Doing battle with Seren will be a far more formidable challenge than anything you have ever faced or will face in your entire life. You are not ready yet."

Mark chaffs at this pronouncement.

"You're just saying that because I did so poorly in *Sleeping Beauty*. I didn't get much of a chance to practice. It was kind of long and tedious. I couldn't even slay the dragon without your help."

Mikhail reassures him, "You did fine, captain, but that was only a hologame, one designed to build character and certain values that are essential for a warrior hoping to take on something greater in the real world, or should we say, in the supernatural world?"

"I thought it was just a game. So what did I learn?"

"You got a dose of humility."

"Perhaps not enough," remarks Mei-Li.

"I remember that it was frustrating to be working with primitive weapons. And that I was forced to exit at times when I was sure I could win."

"Such battles do not always go as planned, captain. We accept setbacks and learn to move on. Character building is rarely designed for our personal entertainment."

"Killing that seven-headed dragon was a rush, and I don't see myself doing that again anytime soon."

"I wouldn't be so sure, captain. Have patience; that's another one of the virtues you were forced to exercise, patience. Be strong and of good courage and learn to wait. You will see Dominique shortly. As for Seren, his powers have grown, and they are not technological, but supernatural, as you have seen."

"So all that mumbo-jumbo was true?"

"Seren's power can overcome any technology that has ever been devised by human beings."

"All I know is tech-power and the so-called power in those fairy tale fantasy hologames."

"That is about to change. Iqhawe?

The Zulu opens the large case he brought in and first extracts what looks like gaming gear, four sets.

"We're back to games?" Mark asks half-jokingly.

He sees large boots, waistbands, and gloves, along with four unusual helmets that he's never seen before. They look more like transparent crowns.

Mark observes, "Looks like the usual gaming gear to me, maybe slightly upgraded."

Mikhail explains, "This game is different. It's called *The Upward Journey*. It's operates at a much higher level than *Sleeping Beauty* or any game you've ever played. In truth, it's not really a game."

"Seriously."

Iqhawe then pulls out something that looks like linen and then a thin rectangular plate of golden metal attached to a gold chain. He sees on its surface twelve jewels and various types of precious stones, three rows of four stones each, seemingly displaying all the colors of the rainbow.

Mark has never seen anything like it.

No, wait! These stones are the same ones that he saw on the necklace they were putting around Dominique's neck in that dream or vision or whatever that was.

"This is going to prepare me to confront Seren? Is it some kind of program?"

"The jewels you see represent twelve powers, many of which are available with technology, but the power of the stones will give you supremacy without any instrumentation or wireless signal."

"Seriously."

"Consider this a significant step up from the *Sleeping Beauty* game. Let's all put on our gear."

Everyone complies, and soon each is prepared to be transported to an alternate reality.

The four find themselves at the edge of a shadowy forest. The vegetation is thick and forbidding, as if it were covering some evil creature, lurking in the foliage.

Mark first looks down and realizes that he is now wearing the white linen cloth on his upper torso and that the metal plate with jewels and precious stones is hanging around his neck.

"Hey, I don't remember putting on these…"

He looks up at his three companions. They are all dressed in radiant white robes with a golden sash around their torsos. Each is carrying a flaming sword. The same type of sword he used against the Emerald Green Dragon, the same sword he had seen Mei-Li wield, and the same sword he and she used in his dream.

"Awesome!" Mark exclaims. "I've never seen anything like this, except maybe in movies. So what's the goal here and what's my choice of weapons?"

Mikhail again explains, "You're wearing them."

Mark looks down again at the breastplate. "So what, do I bash my opponent in the head with this thing?"

Mikhail laughs, "No, one step at a time, but before we even begin the training, let's start with a little...uh...motivation."

"The goal of this game had better be good."

"I think you'll find it more than satisfactory and a goal worthy of pursuing."

Mikhail turns and points to a dazzlingly bright light over the hill before them. Mark had assumed it was the rising sun.

"The City."

"Not the Emerald City, I hope."

"No, captain, a City worth infinitely more."

"Sounds interesting, but I'm not sure I'm all that motivated to fight my way to it, especially with a weapon like this gold plate, and no armor, and for what?"

"Do you see the ninth stone on your breastplate? Bottom row, first one on your right. It's a sort of yellow-orange color, a topaz."

"Right."

"Just touch it, and think about that beautiful princess you rescued in the *Sleeping Beauty* hologame. Remember? She was life's greatest treasure."

Mark does so, and instantly Mikhail and his companions disappear. The dark forest is replaced by an enormous garden with surreal trees and crystalline brooks, exotic birds and strange but beautiful flowers, many of colors that are unfamiliar to him. A butterfly with large, transparent wings flies past him.

Great graphics.

"Mark!" His heart starts pounding. He knows that voice! He turns and sees her.

"Dominique! *Chérie*!" He gasps, runs to her, and tries to embrace her, but he cannot. She's like a ghost. It's some kind of cruel dream.

Dominique seems to read his thoughts. "Patience, my love, my mighty warrior."

Mark is in disbelief. She is right there in front of him, more beautiful than ever. Her eyes are more radiant than any of the jewels, and she is dressed in a white gown. He chokes up, and his chest is convulsing. Mark fights back tears as he reaches out to touch her, but his hand passes through her face.

"*Chérie*, are you only a hologram? Are you not here with me? Are you just a ghost?"

"Silly, you're the ghost! I'm real."

Mark looks completely confused.

"It's me, Mark. Let's call it a sort of projection of my soul, of my love for you."

"Can I never hold you? I miss you so much. I looked for you everywhere."

"I know you did, and you will see me, the real me, Mark, one day in the City. You must first carry out your mission. Allow Mikhail and his friends to train you. You will confront Seren. I will always be watching over you, and the One will be watching over you as well. He will never forsake you. You are a believer now."

Mark remembers Dominique's faith. "I read your Bible, some verses you had underlined."

"I know."

"And I saw you in a dream, you were in a room full of red roses. It looked like you were going to be married."

"Dreams are mysterious, my love, they may not be real, but they may contain essential truths."

"It all seemed real. And you were as beautiful as you are now."

Dominique smiles at him indulgently.

"The world has changed, Dominique; it all happened so fast. I wanted to marry you and for us to live out our lives together. Is that never going to happen?"

"And the world will change many more times before it's all over. For now, you have a mission. You can make an enormous difference. Many are depending on you."

"I only want to leave this life and be with you."

"Patience, my mighty warrior. Patience, *Chérie*. *Je t'aime*, Mark. I always will."

Dominique smiles and reaches toward Mark's chest, pressing the topaz on his breastplate. The garden disappears, and Mikhail and his companions reappear, and Mark again finds himself at the edge of the dark forest.

31

—5—

COMBAT WITH KINGS

"Now, Mr. Great-heart was a strong man,
so he was not afraid of a lion."
John Bunyan, *The Pilgrim's Progress*

Mark just stands there, looking at the ground.

"A worthy goal, is she not, captain?"

"Why can't I just go to be with her now?"

"I understand why that would be attractive to you, but many people need you. Mei-Li spoke to you of a mission?"

"Yes, and so did Dominique."

"You've done combat missions in the past. Does the idea of the ultimate battle challenge interest you?"

"The ultimate battle?"

"Highest stakes, supernatural weapons, the most formidable opponent on this earth?"

"Now you're talking. Is Seren involved in this?"

"The battle will be with Seren himself."

"And with what weapons?"

"He has his own set of weapons, but you will have greater arms at your disposal. You just have to learn how to use them."

"Surely you're not referring to this breastplate?"

"You've already accessed the transport stone, the topaz. You can be translated to any place in the world in the twinkling of an eye. Think of the possibilities of that in battle."

"It sounds like I'll be able to escape something fast, which doesn't sound like combat."

"Let's start back at the beginning, with the first one, jasper, top row, on your right."

Mark looks down at what appears to be a dark maroon, polished stone.

"Just touch it."

As he does, the jasper glows briefly as does his finger, then his hand and arm, then his whole body.

"Whoa! I felt the rush."

"Let's do a test run." Mikhail looks around. "Captain, please go over to that first tree at the edge of the forest and uproot it."

"Whaaa...?"

Mark looks at him in disbelief, but then he reasons that he has performed greater feats of strength in hologames. He walks over to a tree about eight to ten meters high and gives it a bear hug and then a yank, easily pulling it from the ground, roots and all, and tossing it to one side.

His companions all applaud.

"Okay, a hologram, right? This is a hologame, isn't it? The whole thing is an illusion?"

"Not really. Seren is not an illusion, and neither is his power. You will have superhuman strength outside this realm but only to accomplish specific tasks will you be so empowered."

"What's the limit?"

"Oh, you could move a mountain, if it were required for your task. Think smaller for the time being. You have read the story of Samson?"

"A long time ago. I did watch a movie about him. Plus several movies about Hercules. Am I like Hercules here?"

"We'll see. Training begins now. Enter the forest, where you will meet the king of the jungle."

"Ha! You know I've faced him before."

"Except that this time, your only weapon is your recently acquired super strength. Think outside the box. Plus, we will not be there to assist, unless your life is in danger."

Mark thinks about *Sleeping Beauty*.

"And what if you don't get there in time?"

"You will go to the City to be with Dominique. If you persevere and learn to use your power well, you will prevail, even over Seren."

Mark enters the forest and immediately hears the roaring of wild beasts. He smells a stench that reminds him of the swamp in *Sleeping Beauty*. Mark would really like to have some sort of tech weapon, but he feels confident. He pushes back limbs and foliage as he makes his way along.

He is thinking of Dominique, his inspiration for living. Now he has another motivation, to defeat Seren in combat, as Mikhail has promised. As he thinks of his lost love, he becomes slightly depressed, he slows his pace, and his feet start sinking into the ground.

At length, he realizes that he is in a swamp and is quickly in up to his waist. The temptation to sink over his head and die is almost overwhelming. The idea of allowing whatever beast awaits him to just kill him is strangely appealing.

Mark has sunk into a depressed frame of mind and into the swampy goo up past his waist. He stops for moment and remembers what Dominique called him, "My mighty warrior." A call to battle burns in his chest. He touches the red jasper stone and leaps out of the mud. He grabs a large limb and snaps it off a tree.

Mark finally comes to a clearing where he expects to meet his opponent, and he is right. Opposite him, on a large rock, waits a majestic male lion, a little larger than average in Mark's estimation.

"I'm not running this time. If I die, I die."

But Mark believes that he will succeed. The beast roars at a blood-curdling pitch. Mark cries out, like an ancient warrior calling troops to battle. He remembers the line from *Lord of the Rings* before the attack on the Orcs at Minas-Tirith, "And the sun rises!!!" He feels power surging within him, and he cries out like a fearless warrior.

The lion bounds off the rock and charges directly toward him. It jumps, but Mark quickly places the limb in front of it and deflects the beast in mid-air.

The lion lands and turns back toward him, seemingly angered by his move and roaring all the more. Mark picks up a large rock and tosses it at the king of beasts. The big cat jumps to the side, and the rock misses it. It paces back and forth.

Mark picks up another rock, pitches it, just to provoke his opponent. This time he hits it in the side; the beast is unfazed.

Hmm, he's tough.

The lion is studying him carefully as it makes a rumbling sound in its stomach. It makes a slower approach, but Mark rushes quickly toward it and strikes it with the branch, temporarily knocking it off its feet. It rebounds in an instant and turns again to face him, ready to strike.

"Ex-cel-lent," he mutters slowly.

The lion charges, and Mark leaps out of the way. His new strength allows him faster, more effective movements.

Mark circles him in one direction and then quickly switches, hoping to confuse or disorient the big cat. But it keeps up with him and swipes at him with his left claw, grazing Mark's right arm.

Mark is a little surprised at the pain and the blood flowing. He then leaps on the cat's back, wrapping his arms around its neck. He gives it a jerk, causing it to fall to the ground and then rips it apart as if it were made of cardboard.

The ferocious feline breathes its last, and Mark stands over the body with his foot on its head. He feels exhilarated. He has torn a lion in pieces without a weapon. The cadaver disappears.

He hears someone clapping and turns around. It's Mikhail.

"Well done, captain!"

"Thanks, but I'm bleeding. Is this just psychological or virtual or what?"

"It's real, but you have the power to heal yourself."

"Really? How's that?"

"I should say that you're wearing that power. The eleventh stone, jacinth, the bright red jewel, bottom row, second from the left. Touch it."

Mark does so and immediately feels a kind of warmth all around his wound. The blood dries up, and the wound seems to close by itself. In seconds, he sees no evidence that he was ever injured.

Mark's mind is on fire.

He says to Mikhail, "With this superhuman strength and the power to heal, how can I ever lose?"

"That will always be possible, even in the final battle with Seren. Now, captain, it's time for a step up, a more challenging form of combat with another opponent, with another king of sorts. He's not far from here and is expecting you."

"What's a step up from a lion in the animal kingdom?"

"Uh, this opponent is not a part of the animal kingdom. His name is 'Apollyon,' and his powers and cunning are great."

"Bring him on, sergeant!"

"For this level, you'll need a very special sword and shield."

Mark looks at Mikhail carefully. He doesn't seem to have any gear with him except his own sword.

"You're going to loan me yours?"

"No, captain, you have both on your breastplate. Touch the second stone from the right, the blue sapphire."

Mark complies and the stone seems to turn into liquid and melt into his hand. It then suddenly grows large and forms itself into a sword much like Mikhail's. It has the radiance of a star sapphire and a golden handle with inset jewels. It's beginning to look familiar.

Mark is dazed. "Now that's cool." He looks down and sees that the jewel is still on the breastplate, somehow re-formed.

"Now touch the next one, the third on the top row, the chalcedony; it's sort of a baby-blue."

Mark sees the stone; it looks more like a pearl. He touches it with his left hand. This stone also liquefies into his hand and forms itself into a large shield about half Mark's height. He reaches up and touches his head and realizes that he is now wearing a helmet, boots, and a leather belt around his waist.

"This is all the armor I'm going to have?"

"It's standard for ancient gladiators in the Roman Coliseum. The helmet is more open, allowing you to breathe, and your boots and belt will give you a limited covering. You must learn to use your shield for protection. It will fend off anything that Apollyon throws at you."

"But in *Sleeping Beauty*, I wore more armor, sort of like a medieval knight would have; it covered almost my whole body."

"That was a hologame. This armor will give you more freedom of movement. Plus, you're going up against fire, a lot of fire, real fire, and we can't have the dragon cooking you in an iron broiler! Are you ready for training now?"

"Ready for battle, sergeant!"

"Use your weapons well. They have certain special properties that you will discover as you fight. Oh, and remember. You can still be beaten. Don't give up unless you have nothing left."

Mark scoffs, "That'll be the day."

"Apollyon is dangerous, and he wants to destroy you, make no mistake. The only way to defeat him once and for all is to cut his head off and bury it. He's waiting for you right now, down in that dark valley."

Mikhail disappears, and Mark looks down and descends, sword and shield up before him. When he reaches the bottom, he sees a hideous creature standing on top of a big boulder. It's about three meters tall and looks like some kind of lizard with bat wings standing upright. It seems to be wearing a crown.

"I'm disappointed," the beast says, apparently talking from an extra mouth that he has in his stomach. "I thought they were sending me a challenger. Or do you have an army following you?"

Mark responds defiantly, "They told me you were some kind of warrior, but they didn't say you were a lizard with a mouth where your ass should be."

Apollyon struts arrogantly down from the rock.

"Looks to me like they didn't prepare you adequately."

"Looks to me like you've got no weapon."

Apollyon begins flapping his wings and rises into the air slightly. He somehow pulls two flaming darts from his chest and hurls them at Mark. He deflects them both with his shield, and he advances toward the leaping warrior lizard.

Suddenly his demonic opponent unleashes a hail of fiery darts, most of which strike Mark's shield but some of which hit him in the legs and his exposed right arm. He was not ready for that move. The pain is searing. Mark tries to shake them off, but they are stuck in his flesh. He kneels down behind his shield and has to lay down his sword in order to pull out the rest them.

"Jacinth," he thinks, and he touches it. His healing is immediate. He's not sure what to do next. Flaming arrows are stuck in the ground all around him, and the air is full of them. It's not even safe to peer over his shield to locate Apollyon's position.

Then the shower of darts abruptly stops. He is reluctant to look, but he notices someone moving up behind him. He grabs his sword and turns his head. It's Mei-Li, walking through the flames unharmed.

He looks over his shield. Apollyon has retreated back to the rock and is no longer throwing darts. Instead, he is cursing both Mark and Mei-Li.

"I don't need any help."

"I'm not here to fight. I just wanted to remind you of how I used my sword to dispatch our pursuers in the Circus Maximus. This is all instructional, you know."

Mark looks over at Apollyon briefly and when he turns back to look at Mei-Li, she has disappeared. When he turns back around, the scaly devil then initiates a renewed shower of flaming darts. Mark thinks for a moment, and then stands, spinning his flaming sword in circles above his head.

The starburst effect is immediate. Apollyon falls over backwards, dazed and confused; he seems pinned to the ground. Mark advances toward him to be met only with an endless stream of obscenities. This dragon does not diminish in size, as in the hologame.

Mark places his right boot on the lizard's stomach, covering one of its mouths. It struggles but is overwhelmed by the blazing power of Mark's sword, which Mark plants deep in his heart. He removes his boot and stabs him again through the mouth. No blood spews forth, but the creature is dead by all appearances. Mark then decapitates him and pins the head on the end of his sword.

"Very well done, Captain Knutson!" Mark turns. It's Iqhawe, standing about ten meters from him holding a shovel. "You may deposit the head here."

Iqhawe points to a hole that he has apparently dug. Mark walks over and shakes the head off his sword tip. It falls into the darkness below, but Mark does not hear it hit a bottom.

"That's a pretty deep hole you dug."

Iqhawe shrugs, "He dug most of it by himself." He then picks up a large stone and covers the opening, which seems all too familiar to Mark.

The world goes black. Mark removes his helmet and finds himself back in his apartment. His visitors have left, but he is still wearing the linen and the breastplate. He looks down and touches the second and third stones. The sword and the shield appear instantly in his hands. He touches them again, and they shrink back into the stones.

"Awesome!" Mark blurts out with some excitement. "These still work in the real world."

He touches each of the other stones, but nothing happens. *I guess I'm still in first grade here.*

—6—

PHOENIX RISING

Mark spends some time sleeping, resting, and trying to avoid going anywhere. He sits on his couch for a time, trying to process everything that has happened and watching intermittent progress reports on the reconstruction. He thinks that he should return to Dominique's apartment and collect some of her things, but he no longer has an aerobike, and he's not sure there is even any public transportation currently.

"Pinocchio, let's see what's going on outside."

As the walls dissolve, Mark sees a bustle of activity everywhere. Megabots are working steadily, clearing, and reconstructing; some are positioned high up, restoring damaged portions of some of the larger buildings. It's like a huge beehive. He can't see any human beings anywhere.

How to get to her apartment?

Mark then remembers the topaz. It should take him anywhere, in theory. He tests other stones. Nothing happens. Some aren't needed now, and some still haven't been activated. He touches the topaz and thinks of Dominique's apartment, and he is instantly transported there.

I could get used to this.

He stands up and looks around. He first goes to her desk and picks up her holojournal and downloads files. He then looks over her books and tucks her Bible under his arm while looking for an English version. When he doesn't find one, he extracts just a few other volumes from her shelves. He sees *Le Petit Prince* by Saint-Exupéry. He takes it thought he's never read it. It was a book that Dominique loved and talked about often. He also takes *Pensées*, by Blaise Pascal and *Le Comte de Monte-Cristo*, by Dumas. She loved them all and talked about them often. Mark remembers liking the movie based on the Dumas novel.

As Mark looks over the apartment, he wishes he could transport her piano, but he doesn't know quite what he would do with it. With his precious cargo in his arms, he touches the topaz again and thinks of his apartment. His return with his treasures is immediate.

After he lays them down on his sofa, another thought occurs to him. "Take me to Dominique," he commands as he touches the topaz. This time, nothing happens.

"I guess there are limits," he mutters. But he projects life-sized images of his fiancée into the room, one at a time. Each one is moving in some way and speaking. It's almost like having her back again. Almost...

He is about to take a nap when Pinocchio informs him, "Geppetto, you have an Orange Alert message from EuroSecure."

Mark sits up. "Communications must have been restored. Put it through."

Commander Murillo appears in the room and begins speaking immediately.

"This is a directive to all surviving pilots and EuroSecure personnel. Report your status immediately. Full power and secure communication capabilities have been restored only recently. Call in to headquarters for an appointment to speak to me directly."

Mark tells Pinocchio, "Call them."

A receptionist robot answers and asks Mark a series of questions for identification and verification. It then arranges an appointment with Murillo. Mark puts on his EuroSecure uniform.

Several hours later, the commander's office calls. "Commander Murillo will see you now." He promptly appears in the room behind his desk, and Mark is projected into his office, sitting in a chair in front of him.

"Captain Knutson, I am glad to see that you are still alive."

Murillo is matter-of-fact about this news.

"What is your status? Are you able-bodied, fit for service?"

"Yes, sir, I am eager to get back into the air."

"Yes, I'm sure. But there will have to be some changes. Please report in forty-eight hours to the EuroSecure base in Naples, to what's left of it. I have been assured that the hypertrain from Rome should be up and running again by that point."

"Rome is being rebuilt very quickly."

"Yes, I have to say that Seren's leadership has proven quite effective. Of course it also seems that he has confiscated every megabot in Italy to get the job done. Anyway, other EuroSecure nations are not moving at such a rapid pace, which brings me to your new assignment."

"I stand ready to serve, commander."

"Between the earthquakes and Vesuvius, about half our fighters have been destroyed. We tried to put as many as possible into the air as soon as the tremors started, but the covering over the underground hangar collapsed in several places. A number of our pilots are dead. We're not yet completely sure how many are still available."

"I'm sorry to hear that."

"Because the Haze has disappeared or moved elsewhere, it is perceived that the number of supply ships coming to Rome and other cities will be reduced. Many believe that we can begin growing most of our own food again."

"That is great news, sir."

"In addition, the pirate threat is lessened, although not completely nullified. The storms and quakes apparently wiped out or severely disrupted most of their operations. In fact, a majority of countries in the world are struggling to dig out and deal with casualties and the bodies of the dead. For the present, there is a new peace or at least a temporary pause in past hostilities."

"So I won't be flying?"

"Oh, you will be flying, just not a *Prochain Mirage* fighter. We are assigning you to Search and Rescue. You will transport them and give protection and covering for them in their efforts. You have flown a *Typhoon-XR* previously?"

"No, sir."

"It should not be a problem. It is a larger aircraft. It has less weaponry and speed, but greater maneuverability, which you will need to transport and protect Search and Rescue workers in their smaller craft."

"Where will I be assigned?"

"You will report to the base here in Naples, but you must be ready to go anywhere you're needed in the Federation. There are missing and injured persons everywhere, and vandals and murderers are still lurking about as well. Many such people are taking advantage of the chaos. You will have standing orders to shoot to kill anyone who attacks our workers while on assignment."

"I understand, sir. I'll access the training program for the Typhoon-XR and prepare myself in the next few days."

"Good luck, captain. You'll need it."

"Thank you, sir."

Commander Murillo vanishes, and Mark sits for a while trying to process more new reality. He is angry and frustrated; he has a hard time accepting that he will not be a fighter pilot, but rather he will be at the controls of a glorified transport plane.

The following day, Senator Romanus Santori re-appears in Mark's apartment, uninvited as usual. It's a news update.

"Friends, Romans, you have no doubt observed our progress in clean-up and rebuilding. The megabots have worked around the clock along with our engineers. The progress has been almost miraculous! We are pleased to announce a new vision for the Eternal City, one that has come about under Lord Seren's guidance."

"Great," Mark mumbles, "I can hardly wait."

"Food is our greatest need, but thanks to the work of Lord Seren and his disciples, supplies of fresh fruit and vegetables are increasing exponentially. Everything on our farms is growing faster than ever. We now have sunshine and the power of life. No one will ever go hungry in Rome!"

Mark remembers Seren's grape-growing demonstration and thinks about Angela's death.

"Over the coming weeks, you will begin noticing changes, improvements, and new buildings. Let me now show you the 'New Rome' that is rising from the ashes. Behold, the re-birth of the Eternal City and the Sweet Life, the true Roman Peace."

At this, a large hologram of the city appears beside him. It is definitely Rome before the quakes and storms, but several new features stand out.

Mark goes over and walks around it. The first thing he notices is a disproportionately tall building, a scarlet tower close to where Vatican City used to be. It seems to rise up past the clouds. Mark also sees a lot of gold statues and gold overlay on select buildings and along some streets. He also notices greenery, flowers, and gardens hanging from boxes and patios on many levels. Plus the projection shows the Coliseum brighter and more gilded than ever, at least in this holographic representation.

The senator discusses various zones and specific buildings, which light up slightly as he mentions them.

"You have no doubt noticed first 'The Tower of Seren,' which will be his place of governance and a tribute to our new leader who has saved us from destruction and from the Haze. It will be a record-breaking two kilometers high, just to start with. It will rise even higher as his fame increases."

Mark sits down again and watches the show go on.

"Our goal is beyond the Sweet Life. No, we will create a paradise on earth, the utopia that humanity has sought for thousands of years. It will begin here, in Rome, the City of Destiny, ruled by a new Caesar, not like the tyrants of old, but by a righteous and caring leader who is committed to establishing the Roman peace."

The senator continues explaining the design and function of all buildings and then issues a warning.

"My friends, this ambitious plan is not without its opponents, and Seren's commitment is to defend this dream and to protect you, the citizens of the New Rome. Many cities in the Federation are having to contend with looting and violence. Some here have taken advantage of the chaos and confusion. I can assure you that these will be dealt with accordingly! You may have already seen our new police forces. I have previously explained them, but you can access more information easily on TowerNet. They live to serve and protect. Do not be afraid of them. They are your friends and your neighbors. They are committed to this noble cause and will be the fierce enemies of anyone who threatens it."

As he winds down his speech, the hologram of the New Rome vanishes and is replaced by one of Seren, well dressed and smiling, looking beneficent and kind. Mark thinks he might vomit.

As before, the image stays behind after all others have gone.

"Pinocchio, can't you get rid of that?"

Even though Seren doesn't seem to be looking at him, he asks, "Are you sure it can't see us?"

"I cannot tell, Geppetto."

Mark takes Dominique's Bible and goes to a corner of the room where he can't see the hologram, and where he's reasonably sure that the hologram can't see him, at least theoretically.

He sits and reads.

I need to get one of these in English. He underlines the verses that he can understand. He feels that by doing this he is in some way still connecting with Dominique. Occasionally he looks around the corner to check on the intruder.

Seren finally disappears.

—7—

EMERALD AND SARDONYX

"And moreover, at Vanity Fair, there is at all times to be deceivers, cheats, games, plays, fools, apes, knaves, and rogues and that of every kind." John Bunyan, *The Pilgrim's Progress*

The next day, Mark receives a call from Mikhail.

"Captain, I have heard the good news!" Mikhail appears in Mark's apartment, cheerful as usual.

"Good to see you, my friend. And what news is that?"

"That you have been assigned to Search and Rescue. This means we will be working together."

"Hmm, maybe. It's a large unit."

"Oh, no, they have told me that our small squadron of rescue ships will be under your protection. We are very happy to hear that."

"And who is 'we?'" Mark asks.

"Myself, Iqhawe, and Mei-Li, of course. We have another worker, Gabriel, who is from Argentina originally. We each pilot rescue craft. You've seen mine, one of the smaller ones. We also have three larger ones."

Mark explains, "Okay, just kidding. I was notified via text. I've been doing a lot of holotraining for the *Typhoon*. I've qualified to pilot it, but I'm not sure yet about specific procedures."

"Leave the search and rescue to us. You just do what you do best, transport us and protect us from our enemies so we can do our job."

"Right."

"And speaking of training, it's time for more practice with your precious stones. You have not removed your breastplate?"

"Actually, I don't think much about it. It doesn't feel heavy and is never uncomfortable, almost like it's a part of my body."

"Today we need to activate two more stones. So far, you have discovered the red jasper for strength, blue sapphire for your sword, the baby-blue chalcedony for your shield, boots, belt, and helmet, the reddish-orange jacinth for healing, and the yellow-orange topaz for instant transport."

"Yeah, transport, but not just to anywhere I want."

"It is defined by the mission and limited to it, as I explained. That's true with all the stones."

"What's next?"

"Next is the emerald, the oracle stone."

"Will that be like oracle glasses?"

"Yes, you will be able to see what others cannot, warriors in cloak, long distance, through walls, pretty much all the same capabilities, except that you will see even more."

"What more is there to see?"

"You will see into the unseen world, the real face of evil."

"I'm afraid to ask what that means."

"You will be able to see anyone or anything in cloak, and to see further into the supernatural world, you will have to tap the stone, possibly several times. You will see the truth about Seren and his agents. What you see will be disturbing, but the good news is that all your weapons together will work effectively against them and will beat them."

"Like when Mei-Li used her sword against those locusts or whatever they were."

"Precisely. You were permitted to see the threat temporarily. Now you will see your true opponents whenever you need to for battle, and your sword will be more effective."

"And like when I used it in the *Sleeping Beauty* game."

"Right, but this is not exactly a game. Nonetheless, you will see things that you perhaps might not want to see. You will see the truth."

"When do we start?"

At that moment Mei-Li appears in Mark's apartment. It doesn't surprise him. He's getting used to people and holograms showing up unannounced.

"Is it really you, or are you a hologram?"

Mei-Li replies and commands. "It's me. Touch your topaz and take my hand."

Mark complies.

In an instant, they are standing in what looks like an old-style nightclub; they are off to the right side. On a brightly lit platform are several musicians in various stages of undress. A male and female performer, both wearing extra thick make-up, are laughing, dancing, and singing. Stage right is a large mirror; its surface is distorted, like a carnival mirror. In the near darkness of the audience, Mark can see small tables with customers and other spectators seated around.

Mei-Li clarifies to Mark, "Don't worry, they can't see us."

"You know, this really looks familiar. I saw an old movie once about a nightclub, a cabaret, in Germany in the 'Roaring 20s.'"

"*Cabaret?*"

"Don't tell me we're in an old movie! That's not possible."

As soon as Mark utters these last words, it occurs to him that almost nothing in his recent life has been possible.

"It's not a movie or a hologram. It's not real either for that matter. This is for instructional purposes."

Mark surveys the audience again and looks into the mirror. Half the audience members are wearing armbands with swastikas.

"Now I remember. While many Germans played in the cabarets, the Nazis rose to power and pretty much took over."

"The perils of Vanity Fair, where games and fools mix with rogues and deceit," Mei-Li observes.

Mark looks at the stage and then again at the audience.

Mei-Li continues, "Now let's smooth out that mirror and bring up the lights."

The lights confirm it. The uniforms are unmistakable.

"Tragic."

"Yes," replies Mei-Li, "and they are predictive, as you will see in Seren's continued rise to power."

"But these are Nazis, and there are no Nazis or even fascists in Rome. He incinerated a fascist officer."

"You are ready for the second row on your breastplate. Touch the emerald."

At once the scene begins to change. Mark activates his sword and shield.

"Put them away," Mei-Li reassures him. "These are not real but are both echoes of the past and reflections of things that were, and are, and will soon be."

Now that he has activated the emerald, Mark sees that the room is full of smoke and shadows, of hideous, distorted creatures that shriek in their depravity, seemingly preying on both the performers and audience members, both the uniformed and the non-uniformed. Together, they are like an acid rain of evil. Some look like locusts, others like demons from Dante's *Inferno*, and still others like serpents. They are swarming and covering everyone in the room, sucking the life out of them and seeming to derive some sort of vicarious, perverse pleasure from it.

"Think about your oracle glasses and their various functions. Then bring a command to mind."

Mark does so. "*Zoom*," and part of the scene he is looking at enlarges instantly.

"You'll get used to it. It will also permit you to see subjects in cloak, the invisible world, both the natural world and the supernatural world, both human and demonic. Perhaps more than you want to see."

"I think I'm on overload here already."

"Precisely why we are doing this demo."

"Can I turn off this view?"

"Any time. Activate the functions you will need for your mission and they will be available to you for the duration of the mission. Just think 'natural view.'"

Mark does so, and the demons disappear.

"Your vision will exceed what oracle glasses previously gave you, but only you will know that. You will not need glasses of any kind."

"This will take some getting used to."

Mei-Li reaches over and touches his topaz, and instantly, he is back in his apartment in Rome.

Mei-Li has disappeared, but Iqhawe is now present. He touches the topaz, and the two are suddenly on a plain with mountains in the distance.

"Welcome to South Africa," Iqhawe smiles.

"Is this really South Africa, or is it the game?

"It is your next training ground, captain, and it's no game. If you are not careful, you could die."

The idea seems momentarily attractive to Mark, but he remembers the prospect of taking on Seren.

"Die? You're kidding."

"No. I don't anticipate that you will lose, but the stakes are real. This time, you will activate the sardonyx, the striped brown stone on the second row, for superhuman speed."

"Cool!"

"And your test will be to outrun various animals who will be pursuing you, two of which will kill and eat you if they can."

Mark remembers the lions pursuing him in the Parco Centrale.

"Would one of those be a lion?"

"That will be the first."

"And how fast do they run?"

"On an open plain like this one, about 70-80 kilometers per hour, depending."

"Depending on...?"

"Depending on how hungry they are." Iqhawe smiles. "And this one is very hungry."

"I outran one when I was wearing lightning boots...uh...almost."

"Those boots are mere toys compared to the power of the sardonyx."

"How fast then?"

"You're about to find out. Here comes the big cat."

Mark turns around and sees the beast approaching at a high rate of speed. Iqhawe has vanished. Mark touches the sardonyx and takes off running. *Definitely faster than lightning boots!*

He very quickly feels the increased acceleration and momentarily struggles to keep his balance. The lion is gaining on him, so he leans forward and gives it all he has. Soon he is keeping pace and then outrunning the king of beasts. He briefly considers turning around and tearing it apart with his bare hands, as before, but he decides just to focus on the test.

Occasionally Mark has to jump to avoid rocks and brush. His momentum propels him high, and he lands hard, but with no injury or pain. He experiments with jumping and weaving and eventually runs around behind his pursuer. As he does, it disappears and he comes to a stop.

Iqhawe re-appears. "Very good, captain! Perhaps it is not as easy as you thought. You are accustomed to lightning boot speeds, but the sardonyx is several steps up, literally."

"Yeah, I noticed that," replies Mark as he bounces up and down lightly. "What's next?"

"An antelope. He can outrun the lion and can sustain his speed for longer periods."

"Wow! That will be a challenge to keep up with him."

"No, the real challenge is that the ground he runs on so easily will be treacherous, rocky hills, even mountainsides. He never stumbles, but you might, if you are not careful."

"Okay, how fast?"

"About 90 to 100 kilometers per hour. He already has the lead. See if you can catch him." Iqhawe points to some small foothills. "You'd better hurry. A lion is after him!"

Mark sees the pair and takes off running again. He is becoming accustomed to acceleration and getting his balance. He comes up behind the lion and quickly passes him. The antelope is continuing at a high rate of speed even as the rocks that lead to the foothills become more numerous.

The antelope is dancing over the rocks without decelerating. Mark is having some trouble. The lion has given up and turned back. After less than a minute, Mark miscalculates and falls on rocks beneath him. The pain is intense, and he has cut himself in several places. As he lies there wincing, he remembers the jacinth and touches it. Healing begins, and Mark stands up and looks for the antelope, which is nowhere in sight.

"Not so easy, was it, captain?"

Iqhawe is next to him, resting his foot on a large rock.

"I just need practice."

"Which is precisely the point of this exercise."

"I get the point."

"Your last challenge will in fact be a challenge."

"Let me guess, a cheetah."

"That is correct. 110 to 120 kilometers per hour, although the cheetah cannot sustain that speed for long, just long enough to catch its prey."

"That would be me. So does the sardonyx take me even faster than that?"

"There's only one way to find out. Here comes your teacher, and by the way, the jasper stone does not work for this exercise, so you will have no extra strength available, only for running."

Mark looks up and takes off immediately with the cheetah hot on his heels. Mark accelerates, but so does the cheetah. Mark tries weaving and jumping, intermittently looking back to check on his pursuer's position. As he surges ahead, he's remembering the story about Elijah easily running ahead of horse-drawn chariots, and he can't help but play the theme song to *Chariots of Fire* in his head.

I feel great. I bet he'll get worn out quickly.

The cheetah keeps coming and doesn't appear to be getting tired. In fact, it seems to be gaining on him. The ground changes, and he is running over more small stones. Mark is becoming concerned when he suddenly strikes his right foot on a rock and tumbles to the ground.

He flips over and instinctively reaches for his sidearm. Nothing there. He then touches the sapphire and other stones, looking for his sword or shield, but no result.

The cheetah is quickly upon him and leaps. Suddenly it is traversed and knocked from the air by a short spear that appears out of nowhere. It falls dead to the ground.

Iqhawe runs up to Mark and helps him up.

"Your healing stone is now active, captain."

Mark touches it, and the bruises and cuts begin healing all over his body.

"Hey, you didn't have to throw the spear. I had him."

"On the contrary, captain, if I had not intervened, you would be dead. You'll need to practice running at high speeds. It may save your life on more than one future occasion. Now let's proceed to the final portion of this test."

"I thought that was it."

"Oh, no!" Iqhawe laughs. "There was nothing at stake, except your life."

"And is my life worth so little?"

"That's not the question."

"Then what is the question?"

"The question is, how do you see your life in relation to the lives of others? That is to say, which matters more, your life or the lives of those you love? The lives of the weak and unprotected?"

"I guess I always try—."

Iqhawe interrupts him. "Look! There is your next mission, captain. Your other powers are active."

Mark turns and sees three lions in pursuit of a woman and several small children. His mind turns back to the Parco Centrale when he fled the lions while wearing lightning boots.

He takes off running and quickly places himself between the lions and the small group, which is not moving fast enough to avoid being caught.

Mark turns, faces the lions, and calls out his sword and shield. The lead lion jumps first. He meets him with his shield and knocks him out of the air with a deadly blow. The second lion passes him and continues in pursuit of the woman and children, who are screaming in fear.

Mark spins his sword directly at the beast, and the blade strikes it in its flank. It falls over, dead.

But the last lion is upon him and knocks him to the ground. Before Mark can react, the lion is sinking his claws and teeth into Mark's body. The pain almost overwhelms him.

Calling on his super strength, he throws the lion off of him and attacks it. In rage, he rips it apart and hears it bellowing with pain. Once he is sure it is dead, he reaches for the healing stone. His restoration takes only seconds, but the pain he suffered is difficult to forget.

He looks around and doesn't see the woman and children any more. Iqhawe approaches him.

Mark asks, "Did I pass?"

"The question, captain, is rather, was the pain worth it to accomplish your mission and save them?"

"Is there a stone that protects you from pain?"

Iqhawe does not answer and does not change his stoic expression.

"Okay," Mark shrugs, "I guess that's the answer."

—8—

THE APPROACHING STORM

It's the night before Mark reports to the EuroSecure base in Naples, and he's restless. He decides to watch a slideshow of holograms of his favorite subject, Dominique. His mind is racing as he views life-size images of her pass before his eyes.

The holograms trigger memories, but he is also thinking about his simulation training for his new assignment piloting the Typhoon-XR, and about his other training with the breastplate, and about the challenges that lie before him in this strange new world. He is phasing in and out of sleep.

He opens his eyes to see Dominique standing before him, but it's not a hologram that he recognizes. She looks like she did in the garden during the first phases of his training. He sits up in bed and struggles to get to his feet to embrace her.

"Mark, I love you, and I always will. I have been sent to warn you, a storm is approaching soon, but remember that you will have allies. Complete your training, defend the weak, and protect the innocent, my knight in shining armor!"

More like a gladiator without a whole lot of armor.

Mark stands up, and as he does, Dominique disappears. For a moment, he wonders if he was dreaming again. But it seemed so real. He lays back down and falls asleep.

The next morning, Mark gets up early and jumps into his elevator pod, leaving Pinocchio standing there holding out his breakfast and lunch.

"Father! Your meals for today!"

As Mark leaves the building heading for the hypertrain station, he is somewhat surprised by what he sees. Progress in clean-up and reconstruction has been phenomenal. The sound of megabots working is everywhere. He looks to the west and sees what he believes is the Tower of Seren, already standing at least a half kilometer high. He also sees on the streets statues of Seren and other figures he can't identify, all overlaid with gold, and others still under construction. These have replaced massive holograms on buildings for now.

As his taxi takes him to the hypertrain station, he observes more buildings going up, each with many columns and each with foliage and fruit on their various levels. It's an odd look, at least for Rome as he once knew her.

When he arrives at the station, he is also shocked, seeing the enormous crowds, even this early in the morning. As he makes his way to his train, he notices an unusually large number of handicapped people of all types. Many seem to be in pain, some are missing limbs, and others are obviously ill. He hears the name "Seren" spoken and whispered among the normal sounds of the station.

As he takes his seat, it dawns on him. These people have no doubt come to be healed by Seren and his disciples. With the Bolla gone, Rome may soon have an immigration problem.

The train begins moving, and through his window Mark surveys more of the city, more building, more statues, more gardens, and more visitors, sick, desperate suppliants. As the hypertrain picks up speed, he sees progressively less damage in the open countryside than in Rome.

Naples and the base are a different story. Progress in rebuilding the city is significantly slower than in Rome. Buildings and compounds are still collapsed, and rubble is everywhere.

At the base, the aircraft that remain are parked on old runways and even in grassy fields. The underground hangar looks severely damaged and unusable.

As instructed on a text message, Mark goes directly to an area marked for Search and Rescue craft and finds two Typhoons and eight ladybug craft ready for service.

Mikhail and Mei-Li are already there, checking various craft functions.

"Captain!" Mikhail exclaims, "I am so delighted to see you. I look forward to serving with you."

Mark acknowledges and looks over the Typhoon. It's a lot larger and is equipped with rescue gear and mainly defensive weapons. It's built like a tank, ready to endure all kinds of weather and conditions, not as fast or powerful as a Prochain Mirage fighter.

He can't help feeling like he's been demoted somehow. He turns and watches four Mirage fighters rising into the air about a half a kilometer away from him.

Iqhawe emerges from one of the larger rescue craft as does another man he doesn't recognize.

"Captain, I believe you two have not yet met. This is Gabriel Rechuc. He is from Argentina originally."

Mark shakes his hand and tries a little Spanish.

"*Mucho gusto*," he says awkwardly and with a faint smile.

Rechuc very calmly responds, "*El gusto es mío, capitán.*"

They all engage in small-talk until Mark finally asks, "So is there a plan or a mission today? Or are we just on patrol?"

Mikhail responds, "Our unit commander will be able to answer that question, captain. Major Ilde Suravira. Here she comes now." He whispers, "She's from India."

Mark turns and sees a female officer approaching. She comes and shakes his hand. The major seems even more serious than Mei-Li, if that is possible.

"Captain, I have reviewed your file. I am delighted to have you as part of our team. You are an experienced pilot, and your scores from simulation exercises are excellent."

She looks over some papers, and then adds, "For all missions, Gabriel will be your co-pilot. During the rescue operations, I will direct my attention to the team's efforts. Your job will be to fly the plane and keep it stable if we are in inclement weather or other hazardous conditions. Gabriel is fully qualified to do the same should you be unable to pilot the ship."

"Understood, and thank you, major. I'm glad to be a part of a team, of this team particularly."

The major looks at him inquisitively.

"I have already worked with, or I should say, have been rescued by several members. Besides, I know you get results; you save lives."

"That is our mission, captain. That explains why the team put in a special request for you. Welcome aboard."

Mark looks over at Mikhail and Iqhawe. The big Russian smiles and responds, "We have connections."

The unit lifts off and is headed east. It has been reported a storm is brewing along key sea lanes. In short order, they receive a report that a ship has been torpedoed while fleeing the high winds and waves and is now caught in the storm and sinking. En route, they are joined by two Prochain Mirage fighters. Mark again cannot help but be envious, feeling like he should be piloting one of the fighters.

As they approach the squall line, the fighters metamorphose into subs and submerge before it. Mark flies low to the water and begins bucking even higher headwinds. Sensors indicate that it is on the verge of becoming a Rogue Storm.

They eventually locate the ship, which is sinking. The crew has launched lifeboats, but some have gone under.

Major Suravira transmits a message: "The ship and its equipment are old. We make forty-five crew members. Sensors indicate that all are still alive, although some may be injured. Many have abandoned ship and are in the lifeboats or in the water wearing life jackets. Let's bring them all home."

Mark moves in closer, opening the belly of the Typhoon and dropping the lady bug craft plus more lifelines. The smaller ships in turn also open their bellies and release lifelines. All are being knocked around violently by the wind and the waves.

The rescue craft shine lights on the area. The ship also has some working lights, but visibility is still severely limited in the storm. Mark can't see clearly, so he taps on the emerald and sees that Mikhail, Iqhawe, and Mei-Li are outside their ships, probably attached to lifelines, assisting crew members, especially those who are on the verge of going under completely.

Strangely, all his teammates appear to be walking on the water, hooking injured survivors onto the lines, after which they are hoisted into the ladybug ships. Mark wonders what technology they are using to walk on pure liquid and still pull bodies out of the deep.

He taps again on the emerald, and now he can view the sub battle below. Far into the deep, he sees explosions under the water. The Prochain Mirage fighters are taking out the enemy craft.

He looks again just below him, and there are his colleagues still walking on the water; now he can see a sort of glow under their feet. *That's not possible, not walking and being able to lift heavy weights while standing on the water*, Mark thinks. *It defies the laws of physics. Amazing.*

The wind is picking up, and it becomes more difficult to keep all ships stable. The sea is more violent.

Major Suravira shouts, "The ship is breaking up!" The torpedo and the storm have taken their toll. As the ship sinks more rapidly, survivors are on the deck struggling to hold on. They can't rescue them fast enough, and at least three go under, sucked downward by the whirlpool created by the sinking vessel.

Mark looks at Gabriel, who calmly says to him, "You are ready and able to save them. Use the stones. I'll stay at the controls."

Mark then looks at Major Suravira, who nods in approval. He notices that a violet light is shining on his breastplate, but he's not sure what that means. He races back to the cargo bay, which is open, and looks at the angry sea below him.

Without hesitation, Mark takes a deep breath and dives in.

Once under the water, he taps the oracle stone several times and sees the hulk of the ship still sinking. He can also see the three drowning crew members, also sinking and unconscious.

He swims toward them and is surprised by his speed. He feels like one of the torpedoes he used to launch from his Prochain Mirage fighter.

Mark grabs the two that are at the deepest level by their arms and rises to the surface with them. When he comes up, he gasps for air, and the two begin coughing. They are met by Mei-Li and Iqhawe, who strap them to lifelines.

The Zulu says, "We've got these, captain! Go get the other one quickly."

At this, Mark takes another big breath and dives down again and spots the remaining crewmember. He is even deeper, so Mark accelerates downward. The violet stone continues to glow, but he's still not sure why. He doesn't need the light; his oracle vision allows him to see everything he needs to see.

He reaches the last one, who is unconscious, and pulls him up to the surface. They are again met by Mei-Li and Iqhawe, who snap lifelines around them. They all begin to rise.

Once back in the Typhoon, the team is busy reviving unconscious crewmembers and helping those in need of assistance. Gabriel closes the belly of the airship, and Mark makes his way back to the cockpit.

Major Suravira transmits orders through the i-com system. "All survivors accounted for. We'll take them back to their point of origin, the port of Lixouri in Greece, via the fastest route out of the storm. It looks like it's heading southwest, toward North Africa. We'll soon be out of its way."

All craft head northeast toward Greece low to the water about ten meters above the highest waves.

Gabriel asks Mark as they fly out of the storm, "What just happened?"

"I saved three lives, the lives of three crewmembers that I didn't even know."

"Why did you do that?"

"I'm not sure. I didn't think about why. I just felt like I had to do it."

"A warrior who saves lives."

Mark looks at Gabriel for a moment and then remembers what Mikhail said to him in the desert, "So, the warrior has a heart?" He recalls that he said nothing in response. Back then the two concepts seemed incompatible.

Then he remembers what Dominique said to him, "Wounds are possible only in a tender heart." He had never thought about his heart before Dominique. He had only wanted to be a relentless, always victorious warrior. He had no ambition to be tender, not even with Angela, not with anyone.

Gabriel says to him, as if somehow able to read his thoughts, "Captain, you are a warrior. A warrior must be relentless in challenging evil, though it cost him his life. And he must do that to protect the innocent and those he loves. That's what you did in *Sleeping Beauty.*"

Mark looks at him, a little surprised, "How did you know about that?"

"Mikhail told me." He smiles. "Welcome to Search and Rescue. We need a warrior with a heart like yours."

It takes almost the entire shift to complete the mission and return to the base in Naples. After they land, Mikhail asks Mark, "Captain, do you have plans this evening?"

"Not really. I do have a lot of questions, though."

"Our team will be meeting near Rome with some other friends. Would you like to join us? Perhaps we can answer some of your questions in the gathering. We'll all be there."

Mark's mind races back to another meeting "near Rome with friends" that he previously observed.

"Where would that be?"

"I'll come and pick you up and explain everything."

—9—

THE NIGHT IS COMING SOON

As Mark returns to Rome on the hypertrain, he notices more changes. Of course, the Bolla is gone, but now some kind of new barrier with a wider perimeter is under construction. He leans into the glass to try to see as much as possible. Megabots are working on a wall, at this point maybe thirty meters high in places.

He sits back into his seat and watches the city come into view. Still no holograms on the buildings or anywhere. Gold leaf, gods, and gardens are sprouting up everywhere, plus strange statues of what look like ancient idols.

He looks up and sees small, black aircraft, buzzing over Rome like houseflies. Not a type of warplane he recognizes immediately, maybe some offshoot of a Black Raven that was effective in protecting Rome before the Bolla was constructed. Those haven't been used in years, but maybe they're needed now.

In the distance, Mark can see the Tower of Seren, which seems to grow by the minute. On the tops of buildings and megabuildings, he notices the persistent activity of megabots; as they work, all the buildings are rising ever higher.

When he departs the hypertrain and walks into the station, he notices fewer invalids and a greater presence of uniformed officers, a blend of the old Praetorian Guard who are dressed like Massi was and the new Sentinels.

As Mark heads for the exit to the station, he realizes that they are performing security checks. This makes him a little nervous, though he has nothing to hide.

As he nears the exit, he hears someone calling his name. He turns and sees a guard running toward him.

"Hey, Knutson!"

It's Massi.

"Massi! Hey, what's going on? Is there a problem?"

Massi shakes his hand. "No, they're just doing routine security checks. You know, with all these people flooding in. We're trying to establish a comprehensive registry."

"A comprehensive registry? That type of database could be dangerous if it fell into the wrong hands."

"Look, like I told you, it's a new Rome, but we still have enemies, maybe different enemies, but enemies just the same. This is like a new world, Knutson, a dream come true for a lot of people. We have to protect it."

They walk along toward the large exit doors. Massi stops.

"You can't leave until you're registered as safe. Sorry, pal. No exceptions."

Massi pulls out a hand-held device and scans Mark.

"Hey, you're already registered, so you're good. How did you end up with Search and Rescue? Did you check into becoming a PG or a Sentinel?"

"I don't think I had a choice. I was transferred. Orders. It's what I'll be doing for a while."

"Hey, no problem. Lord Seren is eager to work with EuroSecure. Give them time. They'll all be on board before you know it."

"Massi, doesn't all this make you a little nervous?"

"Okay, *amico*, change is hard for everybody. But it's a new day in a brave new world. All these people coming to Rome are getting healed! The food banks are filling up, and the gold... Don't you see how it all fits together? Think about it. It's like...paradise, except that there will be a hierarchy, and there's still time to get in on the ground floor."

Mark remembers Angela as he exits and catches a bus back to his apartment building.

Later, he receives a call from Mikhail.

"Captain, I'm sorry that I can't pick you up. Can you meet us around 7:30 at the old northeast exit?"

Mark remembers the area, where the Bolla used to be. He has the feeling that he knows where they're going.

When he shows up near the exit, he sees Mikhail, Iqhawe, Mei-Li, Major Suravira, and a number of others he doesn't recognize. It's a friendly crowd, and Mikhail introduces Mark around.

"We're going to walk," Mikhail announces. "It's not too far." He turns to Mark, "You said you had some questions?"

As they move along, Mark begins to ask Mikhail several of them.

"So I haven't really had much use for the...uh...stones, but I am a little concerned about some situation arising and not having time to touch and activate those I need."

"Oh, not to worry. Once activated, most of the stones will respond to your thoughts and to the need at hand, except the oracle stone, which just requires minor adjustments to increase the intensity of the view you want."

"Hmm." Mark doesn't exactly know what all that will look like.

"The important thing is to keep practicing either with one of us or as other situations come up, hopefully on a small scale. Iqhawe mentioned that you need some drilling."

Mark thinks about bringing up his previous visit to the location where he knows they're going but decides not to. They discuss the day's rescue mission and what they know about possible future assignments, EuroSecure's ongoing search for survivors in the rubble of the cities and the mountains where earthquakes may have buried people alive.

"You know I miss Dominique," Mark says as he walks along, looking at the pavement. "It's bad."

"I know, but you'll see her again...and again and forever."

"You know that I saw her...uh...ghost. I couldn't hold her. I have holograms of her, too, and I can't hold them either. But they're all I have."

"You have also seen her just before your training began."

"Yes, that was the ghost. And I see her in my dreams. At least, I think they are dreams."

"Captain, let me explain to you a mystery. As Seren rises, the line between the visible world and the invisible one will become blurred. You will have visions and dream dreams."

"I guess I've already experienced some of that. It's hard to know what's real and what's not."

"That will most certainly be a challenge. But it will also be important to distinguish good from evil. That might not always be so easy."

Mikhail stops and looks at Mark. "I think it's time to active more stones, sardius, chrysolite, and beryl, numbers six through eight."

Mark feels a warmth in his chest and looks down at his shirt. It is glowing.

Mikhail explains, "After our meeting, you will confront security forces. These stones will give you the ability to defy gravity, to become invisible, and to project a sort of force field from your hands."

Mark's mind is struggling to wrap itself around this statement.

"To defy gravity with no vehicle?"

"Right, the sardius, the reddish-yellow stone, will allow you to break any of law of the physical universe."

"Like being able to walk on the water?"

Mikhail smiles knowingly. "You will be able to walk through any wall or similar object. It's a sort of wild card. There are really no physical limits."

"And the invisibility you mentioned, it's like cloaking?"

"Better. The beryl, aqua in color, last on the second row, will allow this. You will be invisible even to those wearing oracle glasses."

"And you said something about a force field? How much force exactly?

"The chrysolite, the light green stone, will allow you to discharge a wall of power that will move against anything that comes at you. You need only to raise your hands; you release it by thought impulse."

Now Mark's mind is on fire. He's thinking about the as yet unexplained force field that brought him down over North Africa. Few technologies he knew of could account for that.

He asks Mikhail, "Do you have that power?"

"When needed."

He stops and looks at him intently. "Mikhail, did you bring my planes down over the desert?"

"Captain! I rescued you from certain death in the desert."

Mikhail doesn't really answer the question, so Mark decides to drop it, at least for the moment.

About forty people eventually arrive at the all too familiar entrance and proceed to tunnels below. They descend into the catacombs, deep down, to the same room.

Mark becomes emotional and wipes away a tear. He looks around at the same cold stones, the desolate chamber where he once saw Dominique.

They all sing a hymn in Latin.

> *O Lux beata Trinitas,*
> *et principalis Unitas,*
> *iam sol recedit igneus,*
> *infunde lumen cordibus.*

Mark understands the words more or less. Something like, "O Trinity, blessed light and...something...unity. Now the fiery sun descends. Fill our hearts with radiance. *Lux*...light is a stronger light than the more...something...light...or something."

He isn't familiar with the hymn, so he just listens as the group sings this and other songs in Italian and other languages. Some are sitting on the stone benches; others are standing; and still others are kneeling. Mark is just sitting and thinking and praying, something he's not done much of in his life. He closes his eyes but notices that the chamber is becoming brighter, so he opens them and looks around. The number of people in the room has at least doubled.

He thought he was sitting next to Major Suravira, but he turns his head and realizes that Dominique is at his side; she is radiant. For some strange reason, it doesn't surprise him.

She whispers, "I love you, and I'm so proud of you, my mighty warrior!"

He would like to hug her and kiss her. For now he has to be content just to sit and look at her and pretend to put his arm around her while the music continues.

A man Mark doesn't know stands up and reads a verse from John 9.

"As long as there is daylight, we will do the works of the One who sent Me. The night is coming soon, a time when no one can work."

As the speaker elaborates on the verse, Mark looks over at Dominique. He knows she's okay, whatever else happens, that she's safe and that he will see her again. In the meantime, he reminds himself, he has a mission to carry out, unfinished business.

At the end, Mikhail stands up. "You are dismissed. Please return to your homes with caution and in larger groups. It is late, but many people are still out wandering around on the streets. Try to blend in. We would like about a dozen of you to stay for a few moments." He then calls out the names, including Mark's.

—10—

THE KNIGHTLY MISSION

"Fortune guides our affairs in a greater way than we could
have imagined, because you see over there, my friend, Sancho
Panza,...wild giants with whom I plan to do battle....
This is a good fight, and it is a great service to God to rid the
earth of such evil seed."
Miguel de Cervantes, *Don Quixote de la Mancha*, Part I

Once the larger crowd has left, Gabriel addresses the group, which
includes Mark's Search and Rescue team and several individuals
he vaguely remembers seeing around during his stint with the
Praetorian Guard.

"My brothers, each of you has a specific task to carry out, and
it will be a part of a larger mission for which you are preparing.
The mission is two-fold. First, to protect the innocent and defend
the weak. Soon the persecution is coming, and we will be involved
in evacuating many people to safety in the mountains of various
countries that shall remain unnamed for the moment.

Second, it is our mission to oppose Seren's evil schemes and
lust for blood, which will become increasingly apparent as the
days pass."

The mission of knights in ancient times, Mark thinks.

"Each of you has a specialty and an assignment, but you will work together as a team to rescue those who need it and to oppose the cruelly and devastation that are coming. We are dividing you into smaller teams for now, so you can get to know each other and do some lighter missions together."

As they all stand, Gabriel introduces Mark to two other men, John, who is from Texas, and Tomoyuki, who is from Japan. John is quite large, about Mikhail's height and build, maybe even a little larger. Tomoyuki is about Mark's height and has bushy, orange hair. The groups separate and begin to chat.

Marks starts the conversation, "I think I remember you guys from my Praetorian Guard days."

"I remember you," says John, "the Oklahoma cowboy!"

Mark grins. "Okay, it fits. Tell me about yourself."

"I'm from Texas, not far from you. My full name is John Wayne Anderson. My friends just call me 'John Wayne.'"

"It's weird," Mark comments, "but you do look a little like him in his younger years, except for all the tattoos."

John Wayne does a John Wayne imitation. "'Talk low, talk slow, and don't say too much'... 'Pilgrim!'"

He laughs loudly. "Don't you just love 'The Duke?' Anyway, I really am from Texas, but I grew up on military bases, and then I joined myself and ended up in Rome with the PG. Actually, I'm still with them. Everything is a little disorganized right now. They're trying to reorganize the guard. They've reactivated me."

Mark asks, "Have they tried to recruit you as a Sentinel?"

"They have talked about that possibility. I have mixed feelings. As a Sentinel, I might could do us some good. And I'm all for protecting the people of Rome, but I don't know how I feel about somehow supporting Seren in some greater way. How about you?" he asks, turning to Tomoyuki. "I remember the hair."

"The name is Tomoyuki Kumagai. You can call me 'Tom,' if it's easier. I was in the technology section."

"Wow, your English is really good!"

"English schools in Japan from the time I was small, got my degree in computer engineering from M.I.T., which should explain that I'm not a combatant like you two. I worked in the technology department. They've contacted me to stay on as a PG, and I think I'll accept. Like John, I could do some good there."

Mark asks, "When did you two become believers? I assume you are, if you're here."

Tom responds, "Actually we both were coming here irregularly before the earthquakes and the fall of the old Rome. But after all that, I decided it was time to commit. Nothing like your world falling apart to get you to think more seriously about life and what's important."

John Wayne adds, "Same here. I grew up in church but never took anything seriously. Now, it's time to get serious, which I did after the whole world fell apart, like Tom said. How about you, captain? Have you ever been to one of these meetings?"

"Sort of. My fiancée, Dominique, was a believer. I'm sorry to say that she didn't make it…"

"Dominique!" exclaims John, "I remember her. Beautiful woman. I'm sorry for your loss."

"Thanks, I—"

Gabriel then interrupts them to brief them on their first practice assignment.

"Tom, you have a special tech-pack with you, one you have modified."

"Yes, with it I can tap into the network and make things happen electronically or stop them from happening or make them think certain things are happening. You get the idea."

"And John, your PG equipment is active."

"Yes, sir, it is."

"And Mark has some very special equipment with which he's training."

Mikhail comes over to them and explains to their group, "Your first assignment will be a sort of harassment drill. The Sentinels and PGs are relatively low-key in the daytime, but at night, they are out in force, usually in cloak, watching and searching for subversive groups like this one, especially beyond their perimeter. And by the way, they're also kidnapping people to use as sex slaves and as human sacrifices to Seren."

"Like maybe some of the people in this room? Are they looking for us?" Mark inquires.

"Yes, for people like us. It's all random and on the sly right now, but it will intensify soon. So you three need to move about six blocks from here, fan out, and start making some trouble. Watch the response. Practice working as a team with your diverse talents. No need to kill anyone, just shake them up. Oh, and also, watch for the megabots."

"The construction robots?" Mark asks.

"They're also *destruction* robots," Mikhail replies very seriously. "You're just testing them and yourselves."

"What if they scan us?"

Tom speaks up, "I have a little app that will portray us to them as three completely different people...actually, people who will appear to exist but don't really. That's if they scan us. John, I can leave your PG transponder running, so they'll identify you as one of their own, so to speak."

John, Tom, and Mark go as instructed to a location several blocks away and find an area that does not have too many people on the streets. They squat down behind a large dumpster in an alley, and Tom engages the identity-mask.

Mark and John spot two cloaked PGs just emerging from a building about a half block down from them.

"Okay, gents," Mark quips, "let's have some fun."

Tom buzzes their PG equipment, which goes haywire momentarily. They stop to try to clear up their tech problems.

Mark presses the eighth stone, the aqua-colored beryl, and becomes invisible, which startles John.

"Hey," he whispers, "why can't I see you? I have oracle glasses!"

Mark whispers back, "The latest technology. Just do your thing; think about how you harass people back in Texas."

"Check."

Mark takes off running toward them, jumps high in the air, and kicks them, knocking them off their feet. He quickly relieves them of their weapons and returns to the dumpster.

The two are dazed, sitting on the ground when John Wayne shows up and helps them to their feet.

"*Guardia Pretoriana. Cosa è successo qui?*"

"*Non so*," replies one, who is still a little stunned.

John sends out an alert for assistance, which arrives quickly in the form of a dozen or more guards; some are Sentinels and some are PG. They form a circle and close ranks, scanning the immediate area.

John Wayne sends out another alert but leaves the group, claiming he wants to check something out. He returns to the dumpster where Tom and Mark are crouched.

"Here's where the fun begins," smirks Tom. "Looks like another dozen or so are about to arrive. I'm going to shut off their PG transponders."

As the arriving group aggressively charges down the street, the group already there opens fire on them, and they return fire. All are protected by their force shields, so they continue the charge and begin a physical clash that turns into a melee.

Eventually, some of them realize what is happening and call a halt to it. They become angry and frantically search nearby streets to find those responsible.

"Uh, oh," says Tom. "Two megabots in route. I haven't figured out how to manipulate them quite yet. Their programming is primitive and doesn't allow for much variety."

"No problem," Mark reassures them. "I'll handle them."

Time to use another of those newly activated stones.

As they see the two megabots approaching from opposite directions, Mark again becomes invisible. These particular robots are about four stories high and appear to be scanning the area. He's not sure what these metallic monsters are capable of. Their eyes are glowing in the dark, and they are shining laser targeting lights in every direction and scanning. As they move, they crush vehicles under their feet.

"Be back in a flash!" Mark whispers.

He then jumps into the air toward one of the megabots.

All systems are go.

But he does not register on any of the megabots' sensors. He lands on the enormous robotic head, re-appearing and laughing in exhilaration.

John and Tom look up and see him. Their mouths are open. He has also caught the attention of the PG crowd below, but before they can react, he raises his right hand toward them to try out the chrysolite. Immediately a burst of power flashes from his hand and knocks them all to the ground.

Mark then withdraws his sword, which is blazing, and he buries it into the head of the megabot. A spray of sparks and small bolts of lightning radiate from the head, and the entire body shuts down and falls over. While hovering in the air, Mark aims another energy blast at the megabot approaching from the opposite direction, and knocks it to the ground. He laughs again. He has never known such power.

At this point, Mei-Li appears, looking at him with a scowl.

"Don't get cocky, captain. You and your friends need to get out of here fast."

Mark takes her seriously and descends to meet up with John and Tom.

John says, "You want to explain that to us, cowboy?"

"Later, let's make tracks, partner."

And they leave the area.

Mark returns to his apartment and Mei-Li is there to meet him.

"You're full of surprises, Mei-Li."

"You're not," she replies curtly.

Mark just looks at her with no expression.

"What just happened?"

"What do you mean?" Mark asks.

"What just happened?"

"I just practiced with my team and with the new stones? Is that what you're getting at? Is this some kind of a pop quiz?"

Mei-Li explains, "There are no quizzes in this training. There are only lives at stake and a battle against evil to be fought, which will result in the saving of many lives."

"That goes without saying."

"There is a lot more to be said. But for now, I'll say that you can't have one without the other."

"I don't understand."

"No, you don't. To fight that ultimate fight, you have been invested with awesome supernatural power. Without it, you would never prevail. So how would it feel to be the most powerful man on earth?"

"I think I'm getting a glimpse of that."

"Such power can consume you if it is not matched with humility. You must acknowledge that the power is not yours. The power you have been given has a purpose; you will be able to fight the fight and rescue the helpless."

"Sorry, I hadn't thought of that. It was such an exhilarating experience. And look, they were only megabots and a few members of Seren's security guard."

"It's something you need to think about. I know that you have a lot to process here. You just need some time to sort it out."

"Uh, thanks, I'll start now," responds Mark, half-jokingly.

PART II

—11—

THE POWER OF LIFE

"One can see only things accurately with the heart;
essential things are invisible to the eyes."
Antoine de Saint-Exupéry, *The Little Prince*

Mark wakes up, but he doesn't open his eyes. He lies there for a while remembering the skirmish of the previous night. He breathes a sigh of relief and reaches for the breastplate, running his fingers over the various stones. Yes, they are all still there. He breathes another sigh of relief. He can't remember what he dreamt about last night. Things are going really well so far today.

His thoughts turn to Dominique, to remembering her, to missing her, to think about his most recent visions of her, or dreams, or hallucinations, or whatever they were. All the Dominiques led to a deep change in him, and his heart was further changed in her apartment as he read from her Bible. Since then, it has been the best of times. It has been the worst of times.

He played a challenging hologame and proved himself incompetent on almost every level, except the last, in which he had to have help to defeat the dragon.

Mark remembers Angela, her involvement with Seren, and his rise to power, overseeing and probably causing the destruction of Rome. That, together with so many unresolved questions and mysteries, has caused him trauma, grief, headaches, and sleepless nights. Only the love of Dominique has sustained him. Of Dominique and of her God. Without knowing love, he would not have survived.

Mark thinks that he has nothing to live for, nothing to hope for. He doesn't want to listen to music, to watch any movies, to go to any games or plays or concerts or shows or anything. He wants only to sleep without dreams. "To sleep, perchance to dream." A dream of Dominique. A dream with Dominique.

Now, in this strange new reality, he is no longer a pilot. He is no longer at war. He no longer has a daily routine. There is no Rome out there waiting for him, a city with elegance, restaurants, shows, traffic, energy, excitement, beauty, good taste. It's all gone.

The future is uncertain. His future. Rome's future. It's anyone's guess, except for the dark cloud that now hangs over the Eternal City. That cloud is Seren himself. Mark doesn't know what Seren's specific plans are, but he knows they can't be good.

Rome went to hell, but the dragon survived.

Pinocchio informs him, "Geppetto, your visitor is back."

Mark opens his eyes, startled. He jumps up out of his bed, activating his sword and shield. He quickly sees Seren standing in the room and attacks him with his sword. But the sword passes right through him, and he just continues to stand there, smiling.

"Geppetto, he's only a hologram."

Mark looks at him, and seeing he has done no damage, retracts his sword and shield.

"So why is he here again?"

"I don't know, Geppetto," replies the robot.

In just a few minutes another figure appears in the room. It's Santori. Mark decides to sit down and watch the show.

"Fellow citizens of Rome, I come to you in the name of our Lord Seren. This morning, I bring happy news, but I also must first report a tragic event."

Mark thinks, *This ought to be good.*

"Our security forces were attacked last night," Santori reports. "Two of our construction robots were destroyed, and a number of Praetorian Guard members and Sentinels were brutally murdered. The perpetrators didn't just stop there; they proceeded to massacre the residents in apartments nearby."

Mark jumps up and exclaims, "What?"

Santori goes on, and at the same time projects a reduced image of the street scene that Mark himself had witnessed the night before. He sees the two robots that he had disabled.

Wait! What's this? All along the street, he sees bodies strewn, perhaps dozens of them, including small children. They have been butchered in the most gruesome way possible.

"Our security forces have completed a preliminary investigation. We are committed to apprehending the criminals who carried out this senseless act of violence. We are deeply saddened that this would happen in an era of such great prosperity and hope for the Roman people. Lord Seren himself has visited the site to inspect."

Mark watches a hologram of Seren and walking among the bodies.

"We are happy to report that our Lord Seren has been able to bring back several to life."

He shows Seren putting his hands on a few of the corpses, which come back to life, smiling adoringly at him.

Santori goes on, "But even he cannot bring them all back from the dead. His powers are still too new. We ask the people of Rome to maintain vigilance with us and inform us if you notice any suspicious activity."

Mark watches Seren walking along, wiping away tears, or pretending to wipe away tears.

"Pinocchio, see if you can raise, Tom and John Wayne."

More holographic images appear of Sentinels carrying cadavers from the scene and searching nearby apartments. Santori continues a running commentary and shows more horrific images.

After only a few minutes, John Wayne and Tom appear in his room. "Have you been watching this?"

They both nod their heads affirmatively.

"What do you make of it?"

Tom says, "I patched into the network, trying to figure out what was going on. I'm not completely certain, but I'm pretty sure we're looking here at fake holograms inside the larger hologram."

John Wayne says, "They're trying to scare the hell out of everyone, and next they will identify believers as the enemies, you just watch and see."

Mark scoffs, "So Seren is bringing holograms back to life?"

Tom replies, "That just about it."

Santori turns his attention to his audience.

"Regrettably, Lord Seren has been forced to order increased security measures. We have so many hungry, desperate people in Rome right now. These are receiving healing and food and hope for the future. All this we will give them, but we must also protect the good things that are happening.

"This means we must continue registering and tracking all citizens and visitors to establish a comprehensive database and that we must increase security patrols.

"We deeply regret having to take these actions. However, the criminals have left us no choice. What is happening here in Rome is far too important and must be protected."

Mark and his two friends just look at each other without commenting.

"You know," says Tom, "it's like John says; they're going to be stepping up efforts to weed us out."

John Wayne adds, "So we will need to step up our efforts to protect ourselves."

Santori dramatically changes expression. "But now my friends, I bring you exciting news!"

A new image appears at his side. It's the Tower of Seren. Mark notices that it is now much higher, almost reaching into the clouds.

"It is magnificent, do you not think? Please, make it a point to go to a place in Rome where you can see it in all its glory! Come and visit the tower."

"I think I'll pass," Mark mutters.

Mark and his friends can see megabots at the top continuing to build their way up. The tower has no holograms on it, but its color changes regularly. Most of the time it's scarlet; sometimes it's black, sometimes white, and sometimes green.

"This is the capitol of a New Age!" cries Santori.

Santori continues with a dramatic tone, "In this tower, Lord Seren is training his disciples! In this tower, these who come to Rome are being healed. In this tower, each is being given a portion of gold. In this tower, many thousands are being fed! Is it any wonder that we would receive opposition from evil forces? Some groups only desire to destroy the good that we see occurring here every day."

The hologram of the city disappears.

"So we urge you once again, citizens of Rome, visitors, everyone, to be vigilant, to report any suspicious activities to local security, to the Praetorian Guard or to any of the Sentinels that you see. These subversive groups have advanced technological capabilities and are able to frustrate our surveillance efforts."

"You got that right!" says Tom.

"In addition," explains Santori, "more European nations have seen our progress and have submitted themselves to Lord Seren's leadership. We welcome France, Greece, and Iberia. They have asked that Lord Seren send his disciples to work miracles and teach their people about the power of life."

More scenes of the Tower of Seren re-appear before them and a strange music begins to play. It sounds similar to the music Mark heard from Seren's peace children, an annoying blend of organ synthesizers, acoustic guitars or maybe harps, and high-pitched violins.

Santori continues, "And now the moment you've been waiting for. As I have said, Lord Seren is increasing his powers daily. At this time you are about to witness a new level."

"I have to see this!" shouts Mark. "Pinocchio, let's take a look." His entertainment wall becomes transparent. "Okay, guys, turn on your cameras, let's see what movies Seren is running now."

All of Rome watches the tower. It first turns green, emerald green. And then suddenly a burst of light explodes from the base and seems to disperse throughout the city.

Crowds are gathered in the streets below. They act exhilarated by the light. Mark and his friends watch, looking for some kind of result. Mark zooms in on one of the new gardens next to his building. The trees and flowers seem to be growing at a more rapid pace, and the fruit is multiplying even as he's watching it.

The crowds nearby pick the fruit and eat it, continuing to laugh in exhilaration.

John Wayne observes the scene from his apartment and remarks, "It's hard to find anything wrong with that. I can see why people are following him."

Mark responds, "It looks good for now, but evil times are imminent, even more so than what we've seen so far. Remember, Mikhail says that persecution is coming, and also slavery and mass murders."

Tom adds, "I understand that Search and Rescue is going to be even more involved in covertly evacuating people from Rome. I'll be helping them cover their tracks electronically."

Mark replies, "Unofficially, I think that's what we're getting ready for."

The three friends sign off and make preparations to their duty assignments.

—12—

THE DELECTABLE MOUNTAINS

Mark spends several days with Search and Rescue on patrol. Despite Santori's recent panic alert, nothing extraordinary seems to be happening in Rome or anywhere else in the federation; the team has only been involved in minor rescues and has spent a lot of time just scanning the land surfaces and the sea for survivors, which are fewer at this point. He returns home, tired after his shift. He's not sure he can go to the meeting in the catacombs tonight.

After he falls asleep, he has a dream. He finds himself wandering down the streets of Rome. Suddenly he runs into Mei-Li, his Asian friend, who is standing before him with her sword drawn.

"It's an honor to see you again, as always," he says half-jokingly. "To what do I owe the pleasure?"

"It's time for another step in your preparation to meet Seren."

"Really? I thought Mikhail was guiding me through the process."

"No, Mikhail is not objective enough. He actually likes you."

Before Mark can respond, she vanishes, and he continues walking down the street. After a time, he wakes up. He looks up at the ceiling and realizes that he's not in his room. He sees that he is not wearing his breastplate. He sits up in bed and looks around.

Mark appears to be in a cabin of some kind, but he doesn't sense any danger. Actually, the atmosphere is really quite pleasant. The view he sees out the windows tells him that he is in the mountains. He estimates that the cabin's single room is about the same size as his apartment. *This must be some kind of holographic illusion, or a test, or a dream, or something.*

Mark gets up and walks around the cabin. It has all the necessities, a supply of food, a kitchen and bathroom, and on the wall he sees some basic tools, an axe, a hammer, and even a bow with some arrows.

That will work.

He steps outside, and the view almost takes his breath away. He is indeed in the mountains, and he can see a whole range, many mountain peaks on the horizon. Mark looks down the slope populated by trees and sees a beautiful lake.

Again, he feels very peaceful; there is no danger that he can sense. He thinks that it's almost heaven-like and that he wouldn't mind staying here for an extended period of time, perhaps with Dominique. *Now that would be heaven. Maybe that's the test. It would be tempting just to stay here.*

Mark spends a lot of time walking around the cabin exploring his new surroundings. *For a hologram, this is pretty idyllic, almost like paradise.* He is completely unaware of the passing of time. It seems that the sun never sets, and then it occurs to him that he has not yet seen the sun. He's not sure where the light is coming from. He feels like Adam but without Eve.

Eventually Mark becomes bored by this natural utopia. In other days, he might have preferred it. He has mostly been a loner. That's why he was attracted to becoming a pilot. An escape from people and their problems.

He doesn't think he wants to see Angela. That relationship met a few needs, but there was never any emotional connection, just the shell of a relationship based on physical attraction, parties, more physical attraction and more parties. Plus, Angela was nuts and got even nuttier as time went on. But thinking about how she died and about Seren's involvement just makes Mark angry.

Now, seeing Dominique would be awesome! But Mark also begins to feel the need to see other friends. Tom, John Wayne, Mikhail, shoot, even Mei-Li. Someone to talk to. These feelings are all new to him.

Here, there is an escape from conflict. But he always knew he wanted conflict in the form of combat. Even preparation for combat would be good. This scenario may be a part of the training; he's just not sure exactly how. Maybe they want to see how much boredom he can stand.

Finally, he decides to get the bow and the arrows in their quiver and do some exploring and hunting. He takes along the axe, just in case. He always loved to go bow hunting when he was young. Perhaps he can go shoot some game. It might make a nice supper. Mark thinks about building a fire outside the cabin and roasting deer meat later. He takes a bottle of water and some protein bars and sets out.

Mark walks for quite a while but doesn't see any game so he decides to go down to the lake and look around. As he descends, he spots a 16-point buck. Whoa! He crouches for a short time and watches it. Suddenly, he stands up, aiming, and releases the arrow. It hums en route, and Mark thinks he has won the prize. He can even taste the roast deer meat. But the buck leaps and disappears into the brush, and the arrow misses.

Maybe he can shoot some fish. As he walks around the water's edge, he is content. *If only Dominique were here, this place would be ideal.* It's so perfect already, that he doesn't want to leave.

He looks into the water, which is crystal clear and calm. He does see several fish swimming around and tries to take a shot at one with his bow and arrow, but he misses. Oh, well, he's not terribly hungry at the moment.

Mark doesn't like the way he's feeling right now. *Loser.* He hates the word. He's spent his life running from that label. He's proven himself a winner many times over. Technically, he lost in the hologame. He did rescue the princess, the treasure,

Dominique. That was the motivation, and it still is. But she's not here. The only thing at stake is his next meal. This is no fairy tale. There is no dragon to fight and beat. No princess. No action. No nothing.

Suddenly he hears his name being called by a distant voice. On the other side of the lake, he sees a woman in a long white dress.

Could it be? Could God be so good?

Mark takes off running around the lake, and as he approaches her, he sees that it is in fact Dominique. She is standing on the shore by a clearing, smiling at him. He runs to her, and the two embrace.

This time, neither of them is a ghost, and it feels so good to have her close to him. As he draws back, and looks into her eyes, he realizes something is wrong. She's not smiling now. In fact, he sees something in her eyes that he's never seen before.

Before he can speak, he feels a searing pain deep in his stomach; he looks down and sees the handle of a knife, but oddly, he sees no blood flowing out from around the sunken blade. He looks at Dominique in disbelief, but she has no expression.

Mark falls to the ground, and Dominique—or whatever it is— walks away. He lies there, still in pain, trying to get up again. He finally manages to roll over and drag himself toward a nearby tree. As he does, he notices a large shadow moving rapidly along the shore and coming toward him.

Mark looks up and sees a large bird; he realizes that it is not an ordinary one. It has metallic-looking claws and a bronze beak that glistens in the light. It seems to be losing some of its feathers—which are also metal—, and they're falling all around him. And several of the metallic feathers fall on him, inflicting more pain, but still no blood.

Mark desperately tries to pull himself over rocks to a nearby group of trees. Finally, the bird swoops down to pick him up in its claws. It quickly takes off again and flies toward the horizon, which has grown dark.

Mark continues in severe pain, trying to free himself. He can't see where they're going. He can't believe that this is really happening. Maybe it's just a holographic game. And maybe it's just a dream, but his pain is real. He wants out. He wants for somebody to wake him up.

"Mikhail! Iqhawe! Somebody!"

It's now darker still, but Mark can see off the distance what looks like a large castle. The bird is heading right toward it and in fact eventually lands in front of it. After the bird has deposited Mark on the stone entrance to the castle, it takes off again.

Mark is sure he doesn't want to try to enter the castle, so he crawls away from it. He hears footsteps that sound strangely familiar. They're loud, and they're coming toward him.

Mark turns, and, as he suspected, a gigantic robot, a megabot, is coming and picks him up. The robot has no regard for his pain and does not carry him gently. The walking machine takes him into the castle, where he sees what look like many cells all around a square, each with a large metal door.

The robot opens one of the doors, pulls the knife out of Mark's stomach, and hurls him into the darkness. He rolls and rolls, writhing in pain, but he can still feel no blood seeping from the wound. The robot slams the door shut and locks it.

Mark lies there for a time; he's not sure exactly how long. In spite of the pain, the discomfort of the stone floor, and the stench, he is so tired that he falls asleep.

Eventually he wakes up again, not certain exactly how long he slept, possibly not more than just a few minutes or possibly many hours. He is upset to see that he has not been dreaming, or that if it is a dream, he is still there in the dungeon, and that nothing has changed.

—13—

THE DUNGEON OF DESPAIR

"Finally, having come to the end of himself, exhausted,
Dantès turned to God."
Alexandre Dumas, *The Count of Monte-Cristo*

Mark still can't get up, and he can't see his hand in front of his face, so he continues to lie there trying to understand what has happened. Since Dominique's disappearance, nothing has made any sense.

He thought he was on track and was being trained for a new assignment. He was learning how to use the stones. He recalls his two friends, Tom and John Wayne, and the meetings in the catacombs, and his visions of Dominique. He remembers happy times with her and doesn't understand what that thing was that just stabbed him.

As the days go by—or what seem like days—, Mark passes through many stages of misery. *This can't be a test. Where's the combat? Did I do something wrong? Did I fail?* He has been declared a loser with no chance to compete.

Mark is a prisoner of himself, of his own thoughts. He has been deprived of sight but retains his sense of smell and capacity to feel pain. He is locked in his own mind, swept to one side by happy memories and pulled back like a tide by unanswered questions, a sense of indignation. He has no purpose, no one to discuss this with, no God to ask "Why?"

He has been forgotten in this dungeon. His only visitor has been a smaller robot, who comes in periodically and beats him. He doesn't have the strength to fight back. The robot taunts and ridicules him in an electronic voice.

"What? No friends? No rescuers? No God? Forget all them. No one is going to show up to take care of you except me!"

In his loneliest hours, Mark has called out the names of his friends many times over. He has tried shouting out Mikhail's name, Iqhawe, even Mei-Li. It worked before, but not now. He's called out to God repeatedly. No answer.

He has no weapons, he has no life, he has no hope, and he has no future. He's still not bleeding and doesn't know why not, but he almost wishes that he could bleed to death somehow. He was supposed to go to heaven to be with Dominique, right? Anything would be better than this.

After more time has passed, he can only be sure that he is imprisoned and that he doesn't know why or if this will ever end. He never knows what time it is, and he keeps falling asleep and waking up. He thinks he had a dream about being freed dramatically, but he can't remember. Evidently it was only a dream, because he's still a captive.

Finally, a small trapdoor at the bottom of the larger door opens, and the robot slides a small bowl through it.

It yells, "Keep your strength up! We don't want you to die in here. That's not the point. If you die, it will spoil our fun!"

The robot leaves the door open. Mark is grateful for even a little light. He has not been hungry up to this point, which makes no sense. Now, he is ravenous and has no mind to question the menu or the content of the bowl. He takes a handful and slops it into his mouth and forces himself to swallow. It makes him feel nauseous, but he doesn't care.

"I wouldn't eat that..." says an unknown voice. It doesn't sound like a robot.

"Who are you? Where are you?"

"I'm in the cell next to you."

"You're not a robot?"

"No, I'm a prisoner, like you."

"Why should I not eat the food?"

"It's not all food. He's drugged it."

"Too late, I've already started, but I haven't eaten that much."

"Then be ready for some hallucinations. They will be bad, but don't worry. Just remember, nothing will be real. They don't want to kill you here, just to drive you insane."

"How long will the hallucinations last?"

"That depends on how much you ate. Maybe not too long."

Mark tries to shake the remaining food off his hand and rolls over on the floor. He knows he didn't eat that much. He wonders how bad the visions will be. He's never taken drugs before. Many of his friends did, and he saw what it did to them. He wanted no part of it.

Suddenly a brilliant light shines into the cell, an explosion of the surreal and an implosion of the psychedelic, a chaotic kaleidoscope of colors and images. It seems so real, and yet it can't be. Mark doesn't move. He closes his eyes, but that changes nothing.

A giant red mushroom shoots up in the middle of the cell; around the mushroom is a polychromatic forest. The mushroom grows and bends. On top is a butterfly, no, a moth, no a bird.

Mark is walking down a path. He's afraid of what might be ahead, but he can't stop walking. The clouds are all rotating. The trees all around are also rotating. He comes upon a clearing, and sees a man and a woman. Their backs are joined together somehow, and they are moving in a circle. The woman resembles Angela. She is struggling to free herself and cannot. She cries out for someone to help. Mark wants to help her, but he cannot do anything either. They are both prisoners.

Everything changes color. Then, suddenly a large boot comes out of nowhere and stomps on the man and woman, killing them instantly. The boot turns into an absurd monster with multiple eyes and mouths. It comes toward Mark. Its face is hideous. At one moment, it looks like a serpent; in the next, like a dog, and then, like Seren, and then, like Mark. It opens its mouth and reveals its fangs. It wants to devour Mark.

A storm sets in. Lightning strikes. It begins to rain on the beast, a torrential rain, an acid rain; the creature dissolves. Mark becomes worried about getting acid on himself. He feels a slight burning sensation washing over him. He looks down at his feet and sees golden skulls eating his legs. He desperately tries to escape and only falls on the ground.

Mark drags himself as before, but as he places his hands in front of him, locusts, rats, roaches, and other vermin cover them and his arms and start eating them. These vermin are also made of gold and then turn many different colors.

He hears a bizarre music that is being played at a frantic tempo. He can't identify the instruments producing it. It's loud and just gets louder and louder.

Remember what the voice said, it's not real. It can't be real. It can't be real.

Everything goes black. Mark lies still for a time, unable to move or open his eyes. He is eventually brought back to reality by the voice of the robot.

"So Captain Knutson, where are your friends now? I've heard you calling on them, calling their names. No one's coming for you! I even heard you calling on God. Ha! You're a dead man. You're nothing. But the worst part is that you will not die here; you will just go on living. You can call this place "hell," because hell is where you are, and hell is where you are going to stay."

Once the robot has left, Mark crawls over to the small door. He is happy to see that it is not locked. He flips it up and peers across the courtyard, wondering if there are other prisoners across the way in similar dungeons. He hasn't heard a sound from the other side, so he calls out to his next-door neighbor.

"Are you there still?"

"I'm here. It was bad, wasn't it?"

"It was, but your encouragement helped me through it. Can I ask you the obvious question? Why are you in here?"

"I come here on a fairly regular basis. I'm a priest."

"Okay, now I feel a lot better. So should I confess my sins here or what?"

"That never hurts, but the main thing in this place is to humbly affirm your faith in God."

"God? Are you sure He's even listening? I have been calling out to Him."

"Yes, I heard you. Maybe you're supposed to get something out of this experience?"

"Probably."

"And what might that be?"

"That might be humility. It's an ongoing struggle for me."

"As it is for us all."

"Sometimes I think I'm doing pretty well. Sometimes not. This faith thing is new to me."

"Sounds like something you need to take to Him."

Mark closes his eyes and begins to pray. Whatever he is supposed to learn, he wants to learn. After a few moments, yet another radiant light suddenly appears in the dungeon. This is not sunlight, and it doesn't appear to be another drug-induced vision. He turns, looking for the source.

It's Mei-Li, looking typically serious.

"Captain Knutson, I have been told that you're ready to leave here."

Mark is about to say something sarcastic in reply. But he looks down and notices that his breastplate has been restored. He locates the healing stone and finds it. All his wounds instantly vanish and the flesh is completely healed.

Mark stands up, feeling exhilarated, alive again, empowered, and he walks to the door, drawing out his sword and his shield. With one blow he smashes the lock. After sheathing his sword, he raises his right hand and emits a power burst, and the iron door bursts into two pieces before him.

He steps out and rips the door off the cell next to him.

"You're free now! Come out!"

He looks inside but finds it empty. The megabot has been alerted by the disturbance. It appears in the courtyard and comes toward him, its eyes flashing like fire.

Let's see, should I destroy him like I did that megabot in the street?

The two begin sparring, testing each other. The megabot tries to smash him with his huge iron fists and then blasts him with flash plasma bursts.

Mark manages to shield himself or to move fast enough to avoid injury. He's not worried. For Mark this is more a game of cat and mouse, and he decides that he'll be the cat and start with cutting off a few spare parts.

He first uses his speed to loop around the megabot and to come up from behind it. He slashes his sword through its feet, after which the robot collapses face first. Then Mark jumps up on top of the torso and begins ripping through the armor and cutting electrical and electronic circuits.

Mark moves over to the neck and cuts off its head with a burst of power from his sword. Finally, he plants the blade forcefully in the head, which completely shuts down the monster machine.

The smaller robots do not appear. All the dungeon doors are now open, but no one emerges.

He looks at Mei-Li, "Did I pass the test?"

She replies solemnly, "For now."

Mark doesn't know exactly how to express his gratitude for being set free and having his life restored. He kneels briefly and says as much in a short prayer. It's not eloquent, but he means every word of it.

—14—

RAKEL

The next day, Mark has been called to a meeting in the catacombs. He sees Tom and John Wayne and all his other friends, along with several other coworkers. Mikhail stands and begins the briefing.

"Let me bring you an update about the current situation in Rome." Mikhail appears uncharacteristically grim. "In spite of what you have seen about Seren turning Rome into a paradise, I will give you a glimpse of what his true agenda is."

Mikhail initiates hologram of a small cluster of buildings near the Tower of Seren. He focuses on two three-story buildings surrounded by tall fence.

"In these buildings," Mikhail explains, "security forces hold prisoners of various kinds. These have supposedly been charged with crimes, but in truth they are being held to be used as sex slaves and objects of human sacrifice. Apparently similar holding rooms in the tower are still under construction, but the sacrifices continue on an almost round-the-clock basis."

Tom asks, "Where are they getting these people?"

Mikhail replies, "In the streets of Rome you have seen massive crowds. Who's who? Only their security forces know. There is a lot of confusion, and it's an opportunity for Sentinels to round up beautiful women and handsome men; most are for sex but eventually all are for sacrifice."

Mark remembers, *The same scenario as when they found evidence of human sacrifice in Rome and in Paris.* Seren was behind it then. Seren was behind everything, every disaster, and every crime.

Mikhail goes on, "Everyone here has a unique job within Rome or in EuroSecure. You also have special talents for covert operations to evacuate the prisoners and to move them to a safe location. Later tonight, we will drive four unmarked vans to these buildings. An assault team led by Captain Mark Knutson will enter and neutralize all security personnel. Then they will systematically gather the victims and load them into the vans. We will drive the group outside the security perimeter of Rome where several Search and Rescue craft will fly them to a safe location in mountains of northern Europe."

Tom stands up and explains his role:

"I will keep you from being detected by their sensors and will prevent any possible alerts to our presence. Their scanners will also read you as someone other than who you are, fictitious people that I've placed in the database. Those fabricated persons will also appear on their cameras. The Sentinels have now blocked from PGs most access to their system and its contents, but I've beaten them in that game!"

After the meeting, Mikhail and Mark talk. Mark asks, "Am I really ready for this? I just got back from hell, and I don't think I did too well there."

"Of course, captain! Mei-Li told me you did very well. Plus you have at your disposal the power to overcome anything and everything that the security forces have. We also need you to come on an aerobike and ride as an escort. Your friends in the Praetorian Guard will be driving the vans, and that will give us adequate cover and insure we can pass through all checkpoints."

Later, the team meets at the arranged rendezvous location. Mark is on his bike and is following the four vans. They pass through all security checkpoints in Rome with the faked Praetorian Guard credentials.

As they approach the compound, Mark moves out in front of the caravan. Two armed guards meet them. One scans Mark for his credentials. After studying the read-out, he challenges him.

"Major Stevenson, I think you have no business here."

"Oh, no! This is very much our business."

Mark raises his right hand and ejects a power burst that slams both guards against a wall, knocking them both out. From the van, Tom seals the facility electronically, alters all recordings, and opens the gates. Mark and the four vans file in. Tom closes the gates behind them.

Mark and his team enter the first building and easily neutralize all the guards. Tom opens the cell doors and releases the victims, both men and women and even some children.

John Wayne explains to them that the team is from EuroSecure and that they are being taken to safety.

"Just trust us," he reassures them.

They come out of the buildings and load into the vans. Mark and his group then takes out the guards in the second building, and they repeat the process of loading the prisoners into the vans.

As the vehicles pull away, Mark taps on his oracle stone to do a more complete scan and notices activity in some kind of sealed basement in the second building.

Via i-com he tells the rest of the team to proceed a few blocks away and to wait for him. He taps the emerald again and sees six subjects in a concealed area. He descends a flight of stairs to find a locked metal door.

Time to see if the laws of physics apply, he thinks. He extends his right hand, and it passes easily through the door. *All systems are go!* He becomes invisible and enters the room.

The first thing he sees is a statue of Seren, about five meters tall. He identifies it as a hologram. In front of Seren's image, a woman is lying on a large stone table at the top of a sort of altar surrounded by stairs. She has been gagged, and four robed figures are restraining her hands and legs. She is fighting hard, nonetheless.

Another individual wearing a robe is ascending the stairs toward her, brandishing a long knife that gleams in the torchlight of the shadowy room. Mark knows that he must be careful at this point. Anything he does may endanger the victim, but at the same time he knows that he doesn't have much time to intervene.

Mark decides it's time to move toward the altar. He raises his right hand and an energy burst knocks over the figures on the right. He does the same to the two on the left. The remaining one spins around quickly and sees only an empty room, but he slashes his knife into the air in several directions.

"Who's there!" he shouts. "Show yourself."

Let's see, Mark thinks, *precise placement is everything here.* And he kicks him in the groin. The figure—apparently a man—doubles over, falls down the stairs, and lands on his knife.

Oops! No time to call a medic.

Mark becomes visible again. He goes over to the woman, who is trying to sit up, though dazed and confused. She pulls out a gag cloth and begins screaming when she sees his face and tries to kick him.

He grabs her arms and looks directly at her. "Don't be afraid. I'm Captain Mark Knutson with EuroSecure Search and Rescue, and I am here to get you out of here."

Surveying her former captors on the floor and the stairs, she calms down and finally assents, and he helps her up off the table. He then guides her up the stairs.

As they exit the building, he explains, "We will escape this place, but I only have this aerobike. Do you feel strong enough to hold on?"

In the lights outside, Mark notices that she is a tall blond. They climb on the bike, and she locks herself in and wraps her arms around his waist. Mark fires up the engines, and they proceed to where the vans are waiting. They successfully pass through all security barriers, and even the final checkpoint as they exit Rome.

In about thirty minutes, they arrive at the remote pick-up point and stop.

Mikhail announces that the rescue craft will be arriving in about ten minutes. Mark and the woman dismount the bike. Mikhail walks up to her to give her the briefing that the others have received en route. She seems calm, not at all rattled by her recent captivity and dramatic release.

"Everything is going to be okay now. You will not be harmed. You are safe. We are with EuroSecure Search and Rescue, not with Seren's forces. What is your name?"

"Rakel," she replies with a soft but somewhat husky voice, still seeming slightly dazed. Then she perks up and adds, "My name is Rakel Vardeman. I'm from Sweden. I came to Rome with my brother, Erik. We were seeking healing from Seren. I don't know what happened. We were on our way to the tower. There were so many people. I remember seeing the tower, and then I just blacked out."

Mark looks her over more carefully, as if for the first time. She is in fact a tall blond with thick and somewhat wavy blond hair. In the light of the moon, he can see that she has unusually radiant, blue eyes. Even though Angela had blond hair, clear blue eyes, and a similar build, Mark thinks that Rakel doesn't really resemble her all that much. He meditates on the story she has just told, about how she came to Rome with her brother.

This woman seems strong, but she also has a certain vulnerability about her, which reminds him of....

He can't think about that.

After ten minutes, rescue craft arrive, and the victims are loaded into them. Mikhail turns to Mark. "Please escort us to the Italian border, captain. Tom will give you the flight plan."

Mark can't take his eyes off Rakel. She comes up to him and shakes his hand firmly.

"You saved my life. Thank you."

Mark nods but doesn't say anything. Everyone loads up and prepares to depart.

All craft take off and immediately go into cloak, which will give them only limited protection and visibility.

Things go smoothly until they are about fifty kilometers from the Italian border. Mark receives the message from Tom, "We have a tail, in fact, several of them."

"Keep going, I'll take care of them," Mark responds. His aerobike is equipped as Mei-Li's was, for extra speed to be able to keep up with the rescue craft and most all planes.

Mark doubles back, searching for approaching aircraft. His emerald allows him to see what look like three Black Ravens, all of which are increasing speed. He can tell that they are moving fast and are heavily armed.

Mark maintains invisibility. As he flies to meet them, he raises his right-hand discharges a power burst. They all struggle with the energy wave but apparently have some type of shielding, and two are dropping back. Mark keeps up the pressure on the remaining plane, and it begins to lose altitude.

This is looking very familiar. He continues the force wave until the one remaining plane turns back on a reverse course. Now to find and deal with the other two.

He continues to approach them at a high rate of speed. *I have to calculate this precisely.* And as he passes one of the craft, he raises his sword and slashes its left wing, which sends it spinning and hurtling down to the earth.

The other fighter turns back to try to engage its invisible enemy. It opens fire. Mark is able to dodge the flash plasma bursts. He raises his sword high over his head and then discharges a torrent of energy, which destroys the craft. The third plane has apparently departed the area and turned back toward Rome.

He then receives the all clear signal from Mikhail and Tom. He then returns to Rome.

—15—

RETURN TO DRAGONWORLD

Mark wakes up thinking about Rakel, about her eyes, celestial blue, radiant blue. He remembers that she was a tall, elegant blond and had a certain presence about her. He wishes he had thought to activate his camera.

"Pinocchio, open up one of my slideshows, Dominique."

In short order, a procession of Dominique images passes by his bed. Mark lies there for several hours, listening to Chopin and Liszt, watching and remembering.

Seren and Santori are to blame for ruining this trip down memory lane. Mark's slide show is interrupted by "Today's holographic update," in which the former senator is still giving glowing reports of the healing of hundreds and the feeding of many more hundreds of visitors to Rome. These are followed by news from Seren's disciples in the new countries that have sworn allegiance to him.

Mark thinks about the horrible irony of the whole situation, and the deception, the evil behind the mask. Santori makes an announcement about an upcoming rally at the Coliseum.

Somehow Mark is expecting a report about last night's activities, but Santori doesn't mention a word. Seren just stands there smiling, looking benevolent. At the same time, Mark is thinking about the mission for which he is being prepared, to confront and defeat Seren in battle.

We'll see how long that smile lasts.

After a while, Mark receives a call from the building entrance.

"Captain, may I come up?" Mark releases the lock. In just a few minutes, Iqhawe is in his apartment.

"To what do I owe the pleasure?"

"I know you have been working very hard, and I commend you. I want to supervise another stage in your training."

"I thought that Mei-Li was currently in charge of that."

"She asked me to do this level because I may be slightly better qualified."

Mark laughs to himself. "Okay, what is involved?"

"Let me take you there," says Iqhawe.

He touches the transport topaz on Mark's breastplate. They find themselves in an open area that is surrounded by caves.

"Does this look familiar to you?"

"I'll say! It looks just like the final level in the *Sleeping Beauty* hologame."

"It is almost the same," replies the Zulu. "Except that this is not a game, and it is not a dream. You are armed with real weapons of great power. Your enemy is also equipped. With Mei-Li and with me, you have faced various challenges, but this will be far more demanding. And as before, it is in fact quite dangerous. Even presuming that you win, you will still pay a price."

Mark relishes the idea of a new, more hazardous challenge, but he asks, "A price?"

"Pain."

Iqhawe adds, "In this test, I cannot help you unless your life is in danger."

"What happened to the team concept?"

"In the final battle, you will work with your team and will depend on them, but this is only training. For this level you will need all your weapons, a quick mind, humility, and faith in the One. I will give you this tip. Use your oracle vision to discern the monster's weak spot, the place of greatest vulnerability. It's not always the same with every such creature."

As they are speaking, a large, scarlet-colored dragon appears on the horizon. He lights on one of the hills nearby, spreads his wings and breathes fire. Mark and Iqhawe observe him for several minutes.

Mark remarks, "I wonder why he doesn't attack now. You think he's afraid of us?"

Iqhawe replies, "He's afraid of me. But you are untested. He is eager to sink his claws into you."

"Bring him on," replies Mark.

"There is someone you need to see first."

Iqhawe then walks toward the dragon, and the dragon backs away. Mark stands there, looking puzzled.

"Mark!"

When he hears his name spoken by that particular voice, he chokes up. He turns around, and there she is, Dominique, walking toward him.

"Is it really you?" He reaches out, and his hand passes through her face. "Since I can't touch you, you must be real, the real Dominique, the one I can't have."

"I'm the real Dominique," she replies. "The one who loves you and always will."

Mark steps between Dominique and the dragon. "Be careful, *Chérie*, I'm sure he wants to kill you. I will protect you."

Dominique laughs, "I'm not afraid of him. He cannot hurt me, and he will never be able to harm me again. But I love you for wanting to shield me. Stay strong, mighty warrior!"

"How can I stay strong without you? Every time I see you, you are my inspiration."

"Mark," Dominique abruptly looks serious, "I will not see you again until we meet in the City."

Mark is stunned by this; he is upset, almost devastated.

"How is this possible? What do you mean? What's happening? I'm going to confront Seren. I need you to be with me, to be there for me, *Chérie*, and only you."

"Mark, listen to me carefully. For the next step, you need someone else, and she needs you."

"Dominique, I only want you. What are you saying? There could never be anybody but you. My heart is so empty since you left. I looked for you everywhere, and I don't understand what happened or why am seeing you now or when I will see you again. I don't understand anything."

"Stay strong, *Chérie*. Your mission is of crucial importance. And you *will* need her. We must say goodbye now, or better I'll see you then, in the City. *À la prochaine*."

Dominique fades, and Mark chokes up. He shouts, "No! No!" He says to himself and to God, "I'm not sure I can do this."

Iqhawe walks back to where Mark is.

"Take heart Captain Knutson. The One will be your strength. Keep your eyes on the mission. In your heart you want to defeat ultimate evil. I am leaving now, and the enemy is at hand."

Mark looks up and sees that Iqhawe is gone. The dragon is moving toward him. Mark briefly considers allowing the serpent to kill him. Then he could be with Dominique forever. His breastplate begins to glow, radiant with various colors.

Somebody's going to pay! Seren and all his cronies.

The dragon is almost upon him.

Mark looks up and leaps to his feet, his sword drawn and his shield before him. He advances to meet his enemy. At almost light speed, he runs and stabs the dragon in the heart. The dragon falls to the ground.

That was too easy, Mark thinks.

And he is right. He turns around holding up his shield, and just as he does the real dragon blasts him with fire. He moves away about thirty meters and raises his sword in the air. It becomes radiant, and he sends his own blast of fire to slay the dragon. But the serpent anticipated this move and has taken another position on a nearby hill.

Mark turns and waits for its next move. This time the dragon begins breathing smoke, not fire, and the valley is filled with it. This is not a problem; his stone enables him to see through the smoke as if it were daylight. The serpent is only testing him and his powers. Seeing that he is countering the serpent's every move, the dragon chooses a new strategy.

Suddenly the valley is filled with dragons, perhaps twenty-five of them. Mark scans them all. They all seem to rush toward him, but only one is real. Which one?

Mark turns in a circle and spins his sword over his head. As he does the light intensifies. About half the dragons disappear, leaving a dozen or so. They all breathe a blast of fire, and Mark begins spinning faster. The shield is adequate but his left leg is burned. He stops to touch the healing stone. He knows he cannot pause long.

He looks up and sees that the serpent has vanished. *This can't be real*, Mark thinks. Again, he is right. The dragon re-appears, this time with seven heads, all vomiting fire.

Mark strikes out, slashing at the heads at every opportunity. He severs some, but they grow back. He uses his speed and strength, both of which are matched by the serpent.

This is all too familiar.

Just as he thinks he is about to prevail, out of nowhere, the dragon's front claw pins him to the ground. The scaly serpent doesn't seem to be in a hurry to kill him.

"God," Mark mutters, "what do I do now? Surely the powers you have given me are stronger than this dragon. Help me."

Mark finds new strength, and he pushes up and suddenly topples the great dragon on its back, and then he grabs it by the tail. The serpent is howling, breathing fire from all seven heads, and trying to swipe him with its claws. The battle is increasing in intensity.

Somehow the dragon frees itself from Mark's grasp. It seems angrier than ever but does not spew fire at him.

Something is happening. The dragon is metamorphosing into a giant scorpion.

That's a relief, Mark remembers the monster bug in *Sleeping Beauty. The scorpion was a lot easier.*

Mark repeats some of his moves he used in the hologame with the giant scorpion, but none of them works. This insect is fast, as fast as he is. He leaps in the air and spins, but the bug jumps to the side. He discharges a power burst from his sword, and the bug jumps to the other side.

The scorpion becomes more aggressive and attacks Mark. Its stinger slams down hard and fast, and he has to jump repeatedly to avoid the creature's most deadly weapon.

Then, Mark remembers Iqhawe's tip to use oracle vision. He taps on the stone several times and sees something in the tail, close to the stinger. It's bright red, and it's pulsing like a heartbeat.

That's the vulnerable spot. But to get close enough to strike it is to risk getting stung.

After more unsuccessful maneuvering and dancing back and forth, Mark decides that it's time for a decisive move, whatever the risk. He backs away quickly from the monstrous bug, which causes it to stand still for a moment, almost as if puzzled.

Mark then rushes it straight on, drops down and slides on his back with his shield to his left and his sword pointed upward.

The scorpion's stinger comes down with forces and pierces Mark's stomach, under his breastplate. The pain is excruciating, like none Mark has ever felt. He almost thinks he is going to pass out, but with all the strength he has, he thrusts the sword up into the weak spot.

The creature shrieks loudly and flips over, convulsing. As it does, it extracts its stinger from Mark's torso. After only a second, it stops moving and lies there, apparently dead.

The pain has not left Mark, however. He can feel the poison spreading throughout his body. He is weak. His breastplate has slipped over to his right side. His left hand is trembling, but he finally manages to feel the plate and touch the jacinth. The healing begins, but the pain does not subside instantly.

Mark lies there for a while until he's convinced that he is not dead or dying. Finally, he picks himself up and stands up straight.

As he does, he hears someone clapping. That has to be Mikhail. He turns and finds that it is in fact not the Zulu warrior, but rather his jovial Russian friend.

"Well done, captain!" Mikhail laughs. "You're progressing in your training. You have again defeated the dragon *and* the scorpion."

Mark just looks at him for a moment. "That was challenging. I'm glad to have this part over." Mark adds, "This part is over, yes?"

"Yes, captain, you have prevailed. What you have learned here will help you in your battle with Seren. Of course, there will be differences and other adjustments you will need to make."

"I'm fine with that, but I can't stay happy about not seeing Dominique again. Is that necessary?"

"You will understand everything in time."

"Okay, but I'm going to ask you again, tell me, was it *you* that brought me down in the desert? I seem to have the power to generate a force field that brings down fighters. Up till now I assumed it was the pirates or Seren."

"I can only tell you the truth, I was the one who rescued you. And you needed to be rescued, more than you know."

"What is this other new power that I have? The chrysoprase?"

"It gives you the power of transformation. You can turn anything into something else, and you can make it larger or smaller. Here again, the laws of physics do not matter. You also can metamorphose yourself."

"Uh, I don't want to be anyone but me."

Mikhail laughs. "Of course not, captain! There can be only one Captain Mark Knutson. No, you can appear to be someone else or to be wearing something different. This can disconcert your enemies."

"Okay, I like that. It has definite possibilities. So that leaves one stone."

"Right, the amethyst. The twelfth, the violet-colored one."

"What does it do?"

"It's the most powerful of all, and it binds all the others together in perfect harmony."

"Wow! What is it?"

"Love."

"Love? What kind of power is that? It doesn't seem to fit with all these weapons of warfare."

"That, captain, you will learn in time. But I believe you have already seen it and experienced it."

Mark hesitates for a moment and then remembers. "In the Typhoon, before I jumped into the water to save those people! I didn't understand why that stone was lighting up."

"Why would a warrior do that? Why would a Prochain Mirage pilot do that? I believe that they kill the enemy, but they leave search and rescue to us. Why did you jump?"

"In my heart, I felt that I had to save them. They're fellow human beings."

"And why did you take on the emerald-green dragon?"

"To save the woman I loved."

"Life's greatest treasure. She was the motivation to put your life at risk."

"She...and God...changed my heart, I guess."

"Love drives us to do many courageous and powerful things. Keep that in mind as we proceed on this journey."

—16—

RAKEL RETURNS

Many months go by. Mark has stayed busy with Search and Rescue operations. He and his friends continue to meet in the catacombs. The teams have continued to extract new believers and other disillusioned citizens of the New Rome in small groups, but they have not recently found or evacuated any potential victims of human sacrifice or sexual slavery.

Something has changed. Seren's influence has grown strong. His agents are apparently trying to move more carefully, more deliberately. In the daily updates, Santori is limiting himself to accentuating positives.

Many things about Rome are the same. Mark recognizes most buildings, the streets, and major landmarks; most all have been restored. A lot of the old restaurants have reopened, along with most of the shops. It is once again the city bustling with activity, with traffic of all kinds, but they have no synchronization program, so sometimes it reminds him of Paris.

Mark misses the golden energy dome and a general sense of good taste, which he had never appreciated before. Now, there is so much gold, and there are so many gardens everywhere, and so many images of Seren that just walking down the streets gives him a sick feeling in his stomach.

Security is still tight. PGs are out in force everywhere, but the Sentinels are now most often in cloak. Only he and a few of his friends can see them.

The Tower of Seren has been completed and now reaches past cloud level. Security there is tight; only Sentinels and disciples and carefully screened seekers are allowed in. They apparently don't need any extra buildings outside the tower in which to operate or imprison slaves or perform their rituals.

It appears that Seren is more popular and more loved than ever. Thousands continue to pour into Rome each week. Here, they find food, healing, and prosperity. They are given housing in apartments previously occupied by Romans who cannot currently be located or are known to be casualties of the earthquakes and explosions.

The pro-Seren rallies are more frequent. People seem willing to do anything for Seren, and in fact it seems that there are no longer any sex slaves but rather willing participants who give themselves to Seren's disciples and, for all Mark knows, to Seren himself.

The Coliseum, the Circus Maximus, and other venues host gladiatorial entertainment, sex shows, melodramas, speeches by Santori, and by what appear to be other members of a sort of ruling council, in essence, a restored senate.

Sometimes they hold mass healing services in which the crowds sing Seren's praises. Food is abundant, and no one is in want. Many are commenting that Rome's destiny has been finally realized. Everything that the Roman Senate had failed to bring, Seren and his cohorts have delivered in abundance to multitudes.

Three more nations—Germany, Belgium, and Austria—have joined the alliance with Seren and have submitted themselves to his authority. The result is officially called a coalition of cooperating nations, but in reality it resembles a revived Roman Empire rising from the ashes of history.

This time, however, the Empire has been built not with military might, but with the charisma of one man. There is no civil war or possibility of it, only a small, covert resistance. These are not terrorists, just a troop of volunteers who see the danger, the evil, and are trying to move people out of harm's way.

Within the city limits of Rome, there is no serious crime. Why would anyone steal or kill or even be unhappy in such an idyllic environment? Nonetheless, all security forces remain on duty. It is ascribed to the time of transition in which remnants of the Praetorian Guard and EuroSecure are still visible. As in the ancient Roman Empire, the other countries are generally allowed to conduct their own affairs and maintain their basic cultural identity, although they swear their allegiance to Seren and are under the spell of his disciples. They likewise enjoy a prosperity that seems to increase every day.

The rest of the world is watching carefully. Seren has many supporters and followers in most other countries around the globe, but the leaders there are still holding on to their power and are preoccupied with other concerns. Some nations are focused on Israel, and their armies have surrounded the tiny country, but Israel's defensive energy shield is still holding strong.

Santori very occasionally warns the people to be on the lookout for subversive groups, but at this point there has been no active persecution of believers. Nonetheless, the number of them is growing, and they continue to meet in the catacombs and in other well-hidden locations. Covert operatives—like Mark and his crew—attached to the Praetorian Guard and to Search and Rescue have continued to work without being discovered.

As Mark arrives at a meeting in the catacombs outside Rome, he runs into Mikhail who has been looking for him eagerly.

"Captain I am so happy to see you! There's someone here who wants to reconnect with you."

Mark racks his brain, trying to imagine who that might be. He looks around the crowd of perhaps fifty-five in attendance. Everyone is just talking; nothing official has started yet.

Suddenly, out of the crowd emerges a tall, stately blond with heavenly blue eyes. She's dressed in white, and she looks like an angel. Mark instantly remembers who she is.

"Captain, I am so very glad to see you!" She takes both of his hands and leans forward and kisses him on the cheek.

Mark is uncomfortable. He knows who she is, but he pretends not to, "Ma'am, we apparently have met. Forgive me that I can't quite remember when."

"I'm Rakel Vardeman. You saved my life last year. I know you rescue people all the time and that you may have forgotten. It was dark that night, but I will never forget it. And look! I have returned, as from the dead."

Mark is stunned. He is suddenly assailed by a host of emotions, conflicting emotions. He is genuinely glad to see her but is not sure exactly how to feel.

He asks, "How is that possible? You escaped this hellhole, so why would you return? Why come back here? Rome is dangerous. You must know that."

The meeting has begun and everyone is singing. Rakel leans over and whispers in his ear, "Can we go somewhere afterward and catch up? I have so much to tell you."

Mark can't just say no to her, so he nods his head affirmatively. They both sit down. The entire service is completely wasted on Mark. He just sits there staring off the space, struggling to cope with what has just happened. He thinks of Dominique and then looks at Rakel and thinks of Dominique again.

After they leave the meeting, they go to a nearby sidewalk café and sit. Mark discretely reaches down to his portapack and turns on his camera.

"You certainly do look different than the last time I saw you," observes Mark. "I guess it was pretty dark, and you weren't in too good a shape."

"No, I wasn't. And I would've died a horrible death if you had not come into that awful place and rescued me. I owe you my life."

"It's what I do. It's my job," Mark replies, feigning nonchalance.

Rakel smiles, "Somehow I knew you would say that. You're just too modest."

"I'll ask you again, what are you doing here?"

"We made it safely to the mountain haven. I spent some time there thinking. I became a believer there. I was convinced of the truth by the love and the caring actions of these people who rescued us, risking their own lives, just as you did."

"And it's still as dangerous here as when you left, probably even more dangerous."

"I originally came to Rome with my brother, Erik. He had been severely injured in terrorist attacks several years ago, and we had heard a lot of reports of miraculous healings here. I was skeptical, but I thought, what do we have to lose? But I have not been able to locate my brother. I haven't seen him since I blacked out. That's a big part of my mission in returning. I have to find him. I don't care about the risks."

"Only Seren's security force can access the complete registry. But I have some friends that might be of some help."

"You know, I spent six years as a soldier, serving with the Scandinavian security forces."

"Excuse me, are you not married?" The question just popped out of Mark's mouth.

"I was. My husband was killed in action four years ago. And what about you?"

Mark hesitates for a moment and then explains, "After I broke off a long-term contract with my partner, I met another woman and fell in love. We were engaged to be married, but then the earthquakes..."

Mark sits there staring at the ground. Rakel doesn't say anything for several minutes.

Rakel responds, "I'm very sorry. Was she a believer?"

"She was, and she was the main reason I became one."

Mark looks at up at her. In those passionate blue eyes, he sees empathy, kindness, and a kind of fire that kindles a similar flame deep within him.

He continues, "You said that finding your brother was a big part of your mission in returning. What other mission do you have?"

"I want to do the things that you and your group do. I want to save lives. I hope maybe I can do for others what was done for me. Mikhail seems happy that I've returned to aid in the effort. I served in a Special Forces unit in Sweden. I'm well-trained and know how to use technology and weapons."

Rakel pauses for a few seconds. "Another question? Don't answer if you don't want to."

Mark just looks at her. "Shoot."

"They tell me that you have certain special powers, but no one has explained any details. The night you rescued me I saw you do things I couldn't explain or understand. Of course I was a little out of it. Can you refresh my memory or enlighten me?"

"I have some powers, but I don't understand them myself. I know that I have a mission for which I'm in training. I don't know how long it will take. In the meantime, I'm committed to rescuing people and evacuating them from this evil place."

Rakel smiles, "I want to be a part of that, a part of your team. Here I'm only a civilian and have no job or official standing. I think that could be useful."

Mark listens intently to everything she says. He's looking into her eyes and sees sincerity, among other things. Maybe he's now looking a little too long.

"Okay, I have another question."

"Okay."

"How do you speak English so well?"

"That's classified, captain!" She then laughs, "Actually, I studied at Oxford. I was in Scandinavian Special Forces, military intelligence, and English was vital for that mission."

"I don't hear any British accent. You sound like an American."

"Ha! That's what they said at Oxford. I'm sure I've been corrupted by all the American movies I've watched since I was a kid."

Mark laughs. He feels guilty for laughing, a little embarrassed for enjoying her company so much.

As they part, they decide they will get together again after the next meeting in the catacombs in just a few days.

"Mikhail told me that a new mission is being planned," says Rakel. "I want to be a part."

—17—

BLACKBELT WITH BLACK SASH

The church in Rome is growing, and everyone knows that the persecution is coming. During this period of relative peace, the covert teams continue to move small groups out of Rome, transporting them to safer areas in the mountains to the north.

Mikhail has asked Rakel to become a regular part of the team and to work with Mark. Of course, Mark has worked with women before, but this one makes him a little uneasy.

On their first mission together, Mark and Rakel are each riding aerobikes, escorting several vans. They are inconspicuous, low-key; the vans are like hundreds of others going many different directions in the city of Rome. Mark takes the lead, and the vans follow him. Rakel brings up the rear. Everything seems routine until they leave the city and reach the remote pickup point.

As they start unloading the vans and waiting for the evacuation craft, Tom warns Mark on i-com, "I'm reading six individuals, all males, armed, and headed this way. I've disabled their weapons. And by the way, they're Aussies, judging by their accents."

In just a few moments, they are approached by the six men. Mark looks them over. They are not Sentinels, nor are they Praetorian Guard members.

One of the men says, "What 'a we got heeyah? Whatchya doin'?"

Mark replies, "Just routine transport, friend."

"Ah! A yank! Right, just our luck, a bloke who speaks the King's English." They all laugh.

"Hey, mate, we want to see what ya have in the vans theyah. Ya won't mind, now will ya?"

Mark responds firmly, "Just people, we're transporting people. Go your way. We don't want any trouble."

"Hey, boys, 'e's givin' orders to us. Tellin' us to rack off. Mate, you and ya friends had bloody well rack off yourselves. Ya're big talk. Ya got no weapons."

Mark retorts defiantly, "Weapons? No, we ain't got no weapons. We don't need no stinking weapons!"

John Wayne gets out of one of the vans and comes over to see if Mark needs assistance. Rakel moves closer as well.

The Aussie looks at John. "Oh! Reinforcements, eh? Who the bloody hell are you?"

"I'm John Wayne."

They all burst out laughing.

"Funny man, eh? I count six of us and two of you." They all draw their weapons. "Plus six of these."

Mark has a sense of how this is going to go down, but he doesn't want to use his powers unless he absolutely has to. Predictably, the atmosphere becomes more intense.

The men quickly discover that their blasters are useless.

Mark looks at John Wayne and asks, "What you think John? Three for you and three for me?"

The six thugs are provoked by this and become agitated. Then Rakel walks up and adds, "I'll take two or even more if you two can't handle the rest."

None of the six takes Rakel seriously, and they immediately face off with John Wayne and Mark.

Then Rakel makes her move. She jumps and delivers a stomp-kick to the chest of the one closest to her and then a sweep kick to the next, knocking them both to the ground.

The group—including Mark and John Wayne—is shocked and distracted for about a second. In the next second, John Wayne tackles the two on his side and wrestles them to the ground. Then Mark, changing his mind, raises his hands, and discharges a power burst that knocks over the remaining two.

The thugs are dazed and groaning as Mark and John Wayne put restraints and blindfolds on them. As they work, they look over at Rakel curiously.

Rakel brushes herself off, and apologizes, "Sorry that took so long. I have a black belt in kickboxing. Of course, the aerobike boots help a little."

Mark asks, "A black belt?"

She replies, "Yeah, a black belt with a black sash. I told you I was in Special Forces for Scandinavian Security. What do you think I did? Give back rubs? I guess I'm a little rusty. But hey, nice touch with the take-off from *The Treasure of the Sierra Madre*."

"The what?"

"Bogart film, 1948. The Mexican guy says that, except it's 'badges? We ain't got no badges.' You know."

"No, I guess I never knew where that came from."

The rescue craft arrive, load up, and take off. Mark escorts them north, but Rakel does not follow because she has no weapons.

Over time Rakel repeatedly proves herself a valuable asset to the team and to Mark. He respects her as a soldier and fellow fighter. He enjoys working with her. He enjoys it a lot.

The two start working out together several times a week; Rakel's work-outs are unusual, very different from those he used to have with Angela.

When they arrive at a local gym, they run together on the moving floor. They lift weights and fence, but Rakel also loves to tap-dance and kick box, both at the same time. And while doing these, she listens to jazz, selections from the more than one hundred years of the art, from "jump and jive" to "gypsy jazz." She puts on her audio earpieces and livens things up.

Mark can't really keep up with her, so he just tries to stay out of her way. He's already seen what she can do with her feet.

"Isn't that a little dangerous?" Mark asks. "With the metal on those tap shoes, a slick floor, and your fast movements, you could slip and hurt yourself."

"Ah, but that's the real test. Can you react fast, maintain your balance, and be ready for sudden changes in footing?"

Mark is mystified.

In fencing, Rakel is very good and very competitive. They wear the standard protective gear, but she is aggressive and fast. Mark would like to say that he lets her win, but her skills match his, and she seems to enjoy scoring on him.

"This is all in fun, right?" He asks, only half joking.

"Of course!" she exclaims, laughing. "I hope you're not taking it too seriously."

"Of course not."

After workouts, they often go to an outdoor café and talk. Mark has his usual Coca-Cola, and she always orders some exotic tea, a different one every time.

After a few weeks of meeting and chatting about superficial topics, Rakel asks him, "Tell me more about you, Mark."

"Not a whole lot to tell, I'm afraid. I've already mentioned my family back in Oklahoma. How I served there in the U.S. for a time and then came to Rome."

"I'd like to hear more about Dominique, if you feel comfortable talking about her."

Mark becomes pensive for a moment.

She adds, "You don't have to, if it's still hard."

Mark reflects for another moment.

"Dominique opened me up to so many things in my past, the love for music that my mother instilled in me. With Dominique I was able to feel again, to feel emotions like a normal human being. I cried for the first time since I was a kid. She also opened me up to faith in God. I think I've mentioned that. You know, I loved her...so...." He chokes up.

"Yes, I can tell. She must've been a wonderful woman. I bet you think about her a lot and even dream about her."

Mark thinks, *You have no idea.*

He turns to her, "Tell me more about yourself. About your husband and your life back in Sweden."

"I could get choked up, too. My husband and I served in the military together. He was tall and strong, a good soldier and a good husband. We never had children together. Can I assume that you have no children?"

"No, none with Angela, my first, and Dominique and I never even got married. I guess that children were a part of the dream we shared. It just never happened."

Rakel also meditates for a moment. "We were busy with our careers. The early years were fairly peaceful, but then the terrorist attacks started again. So many innocent people were killed. My husband died in a firefight. My brother was injured in a terrorist explosion. My whole world fell apart."

Mark watches Rakel carefully as she speaks. As far as he can tell, she is not wearing makeup. Those starry blue eyes sparkle and flash. As she talks, she reveals her fire and passion for life. She is, in a word, intense about almost everything.

Mark finally adds, "I hope I can help you find your brother. It's no easy task nowadays. So many people are coming into Rome, and so many are disappearing, for many different reasons."

"Thank you for the offer. I am determined to find him. I will find him if I die trying."

"Don't say that. I will be there for you. I am specially equipped to help you."

"I already asked you about the special powers you have. And I know I've seen some. That burst from the hand thing. What other powers do you have? Sorry, I'm just really curious."

"As I told you, I have been given certain capabilities and training that will prepare me for a confrontation of some kind. I don't think I mentioned more than that. I am to take on Seren himself, to fight him and to kill him."

"Really? When does that happen?"

"I'm not sure. I think I still have a lot of preparation to do."

"I'd like to help you prepare for the battle and maybe be there when it happens."

"I don't know about that."

But Mark remembers what Dominique told him, that someone needs him, and that he will need her.

After a few more weeks, Rakel suggests that they have dinner together.

"You have a favorite restaurant?" Mark asks.

"Restaurant? I was thinking that I could come to your apartment. I've been living in temporary quarters, sharing expenses with a Danish lady I met. Your apartment has some electronics, no?"

"Yes, it's fully equipped. I even have *Holovision 500.*"

"Then how about I come and bring dinner and entertainment?"

"What would that look like?"

"Shush! It's going to be a surprise. When do I come by?"

—18—

CASABLANCA, REVISITED

At 6:30, Mark is anxiously awaiting Rakel's arrival. He is a bit nervous, because he doesn't know quite what to expect. He's also uneasy because he's not completely certain where this relationship might go. He would definitely like for it to go deeper, but he's not sure that he's ready for that.

Mark tries to straighten up the place, and he sets the table. He even pulls an old candle out of a drawer, lights it, and places it in the middle.

When Rakel arrives at his door, she bumps it with her knees. Mark opens the door, and she walks in carrying a box of pizza, a large bottle of Coke, an umbrella, and wearing an old-fashioned hat. He can only wonder what will happen next.

"Nice place you have here," Rakel says exuberantly, "It's a little Spartan, but I expected that."

Rakel is vivacious and enthusiastic about almost everything, a quality that Mark likes.

She continues, "Oh, I see you set the table. But no need. Let's just break up the pizza and pour ourselves a little Coca-Cola and talk."

Mark tries to help her take the box and bottle over to the table next to the kitchen.

"Oh, no, silly boy, let's just sit on the floor with our backs up against the couch."

So they sit, eat pizza slices, drink Coke, and chat. They're listening to Louie Armstrong and Ella Fitzgerald sing "Dream a Little Dream of Me."

Mark says to her, "You know, a lot of nice restaurants are up and running again."

"Yes, but there's nothing like pizza made in Italy, relaxing in the comfort of your own home. I mean, I haven't been in Italy all that long. And the pizza and the pasta in general are excellent. Quite a treat. Not sure I could ever get tired of the cuisine here."

"So what subjects are we going to cover tonight?" Mark asks. Rakel always seems full of surprises.

She wrinkles her brow. "We don't have to *cover* anything. It's nice just to be here with you."

"You haven't told me much about your brother. What was his name again?"

"Erik. He's four years younger than me. He was always such a good kid. You know what he was doing when that terrorist bomb went off? He was training to be a policeman. He really wanted to help people and protect them. He was at a gym, doing an extra work-out. Needless to say, that dream ended. The doctors couldn't do anything for him. His injuries were too severe. He lost his left leg and his left arm, plus the scarring and other damage."

"So you thought that Seren could heal him?"

"We had no other hope. We had heard a lot of stories. I finally decided to make the trip."

"And your parents?"

"They passed away years ago. Of natural causes. It was just Erik and me. He really helped me a lot after my husband's death."

"I wonder," Mark thinks out loud, "how we might get some information about Erik's whereabouts?"

Rakel speculates, "I bet they know something at the Tower of Seren, but who wants to go there?"

Mark is thoughtful for a moment. "I think it might be worth the trip. We'll just have to make some careful preparations before going. Our friend, Tom, can check the database on you, and be sure there's no information about your activities since arriving in Rome or since you've returned."

"Considering what we know now, the idea of going into the tower gives me the creeps."

They continue to talk and tell each other stories about their lives before they met. They laugh, or should we say that Mark laughs a lot at the funny, quirky things that Rakel says.

He remarks, "There certainly has been some good entertainment tonight."

"Oh, the real fun is about to begin!"

Rakel goes over to his entertainment system and plugs her portapack into it.

"Just as I thought, you don't have these movies. Wow! You certainly like action-adventure, science fiction, and fantasy. This won't be any of those. I love old movies, really old movies. So this first little clip will only be in 2-D, but it is in color!"

Rakel picks up the umbrella and the hat she brought. Before the show begins, she steps to the left of the screen, and the entertainment center starts producing... rain. She doesn't open up her umbrella quite yet. She's not getting wet of course, but the virtual rain is falling. After only a few seconds, Gene Kelly appears on the screen, singing...in the rain.

Rakel mimics his dance, his moves, when he opens and closes his umbrella. She can't jump on a light pole, but she makes the movement. She sings laughingly, almost deliriously. Mark has never seen anyone look quite so happy. *And this woman has had a really tough time in her life.*

Then Gene Kelly starts to tap-dance, and there is Rakel in Mark's apartment, tap-dancing beside him in perfect sync.

When she finishes, Mark applauds "I think I may have seen that movie quite a few years ago. That thing has to be over a hundred years old by now. I have to say that I know I haven't ever seen this particular version."

"I love the song, the movie, and so many classic movies just like it."

"Okay, what's next for entertainment?"

"Next is..." She makes a selection on her portapack. The 2-D movie begins; it's *Casablanca*.

Mark laughs out loud.

"*Casablanca*? I guess that's the logical follow-up to *Singing in the Rain*."

"I love those impossible love stories. Don't ask me why. I also think there's a certain relationship between this movie and what is happening right now in Rome. Have you ever seen it?"

"Oh, just excerpts. I may have seen the whole thing, but I can't remember. Doesn't it take place in North Africa? Isn't it about World War II?"

"Yes, and you'll love it! Adventure, intrigue, and romance. And a story about refugees trying to escape the Nazis. They go to Casablanca, unoccupied France, and try to get visas to Portugal and eventually to America. And in the middle of it all, a love story. Think about it, dreams and destiny in a dangerous city."

"But you said it was one of those *impossible* love stories."

"Bogart plays this Rick Blaine guy; he owns a nightclub in Casablanca. Enter his old flame Ilsa, that's Ingrid Bergman. She comes to town with her husband, uh, something Laszlo. He has the Germans on his tail. They go to Rick thinking that he can help them get exit visas. So there are some sparks between Bogart and Bergman, and okay, no more spoilers, just watch it!"

They enjoy the film together. When it is finished, Mark looks at Rakel, "Here's looking at you, kid."

"Isn't it a great film?"

"Yes, it is. I enjoyed it, but I think it's a little bit more than just another impossible love story."

"Did you feel the electricity between Bogart and Bergman?"

"I did," Mark answers. He thinks, *I'm feeling a little electricity right now, being with you.* "But it is more than that. I liked the intrigue with the Nazis. It's weird because they were frustrated throughout. They couldn't seem to get Bogart or that...what was his name?"

"Laszlo."

"Yeah, him. Bogart's courage is the key. It's not a war film per se, you know, with battle scenes. But Bogie had guts, moral guts to put himself out there, take a risk, to help them escape."

"Like we said, that's what we're doing here in Rome. We're rescuing people from the evil of Seren."

"From certain death, captivity, torture, and who knows what else?"

"I didn't like Lazlo all that much. I could just wish that Bogie and Ingrid could have gotten together somehow."

"You're a dreamer."

"Yes, I am. And you?"

"I've never been much of a dreamer, at night or in the daytime, but lately, I dream a lot."

Then Mark looks at her more carefully and says, "Actually, you look like Ingrid Bergman... At least a little."

"Do you really think so? Oh, thank you! I wish my parents had named me Ingrid. She is so beautiful."

They both sit and look at the blank screen for a few moments.

"Mark, I don't want to offend you, but has anyone ever told you that you look a little like Seren? I've never seen him in person, I'm just judging by his holograms."

Mark rolls his eyes. "I don't see it. But, yes, at least one person has mentioned that."

"Maybe if you let your beard grow."

—19—

THE TOWER OF SEREN

Mark asks Tom about tapping into the registry.

He responds, "So far, the Praetorian Guard has had access to most routine information in the database. I don't know how long that's going to last. It seems that they're in the process of building a firewall, especially around the Tower of Seren."

"So what about Rakel? What does it say about her?"

"Just her arrival, and it notes that she was accompanied by her brother, gives his name, Erik, and their country of origin, Sweden. It observes that he had apparently sustained severe injuries. There's a picture of both of them. No cautions or information about their movements."

"Nothing about her incarceration?"

"No, nothing. I'm pretty sure I wiped pertinent info in their records the night we rescued Rakel, but you'd still better be careful if you start snooping around asking questions over there."

"I think it's the only way. I'm certain we'll find some answers in the tower. It's also about time I went to see what's going on. This is a pretty good reason to pay Seren a visit."

"The place is a mystery. A lot of areas are open to the public, and we can easily get a lot of superficial information related to the tower itself. The upper levels are dark. I'm not sure if they're just still under construction, or they have blanked them out to hide the human sacrifices."

"If they have built a firewall, I trust that you can crack it."

"Do you doubt? It will take some time, but they can't hide anything from me for long!"

Mark and Rakel go to the tower and stand in line for about an hour before they are even allowed to enter. They are scanned and cleared. As they walk in, Mark gains an appreciation of how majestic it is inside, at least the ground-floor. He hears that same strange music, this time with flutes, violins, and synthesizers.

The Great Hall is huge and is bustling with activity. Mark estimates that there might be a thousand visitors there today. Individuals and groups are treated very cordially and are routed to various windows, depending on their need.

In the center is what looks like altar, with a gold statue of Seren at the top. As usual he has a benign expression on his face and is holding his hands out, palms up. From between his hands is flowing fountain of water which fills a pool all around the base. Lush vegetation surrounds the water.

One of the assistants approaches them and asks, "Welcome to Serenity Tower. How may we be of service?"

Mark speaks up, "This lady is looking for her brother. They came together—"

The assistant politely interrupts, looking at the readout on a device
he is carrying.

"Yes, excuse me, you are Captain Mark Knutson, EuroSecure Search and Rescue, and she is Rakel Vardeman, and your brother, Erik. It appears you arrive last year and were seeking healing from Lord Seren."

Almost as quickly as he speaks the name "Seren," several people nearby hear it, look at Mark, and erroneously conclude that he is in fact Seren.

One of them cries out, "It's Lord Seren! He's here!"

Others shout the same. In a short order, the whole ground-floor is in an uproar. Most are yelling, and many are pressing in, trying to reach Mark, who looks bewildered.

Sentinels quickly make their way through the crowd and hustle Mark and Rakel to a private room on the side. The assistants try to calm the crowd and to correct the erroneous impression.

Mark and Rakel are treated very courteously, but Mark notices that after only a few minutes, six Sentinels have joined them in the room. No one is saying anything.

After a few more moments, a door opens and two more Sentinels enter, followed by Seren himself. Mark and Rakel stand.

Seren looks them over carefully and makes a bowing gesture, "I am ever your humble servant."

Mark just nods his head, and Rakel does nothing.

"What is the problem?" asks Seren.

"My Lord Seren," explains one of the assistants. "A few moments ago, we had a disturbance in the Great Hall. Apparently someone mistook this gentleman for you. Of course, there was so much excitement that you might be near that things got out of hand very quickly. Their names, my Lord, are Captain Mark Knutson and Ms. Rakel Vardeman."

As he is listening to the explanation, Seren is studying both of them carefully. He looks directly at Mark and glances down at his chest several times. *Can he see or sense the breastplate?* Mark wonders.

"Do we know each other?"

Mark cannot bring himself to address Seren as Lord, so he replies in a more military fashion, "Sir, we met some time ago. I came to one of your meetings at the invitation of Ms. Angela Pesci."

Seren registers surprise and seems to remember, "Ah, yes! The pilot. Yes, yes, I do remember now. You were with EuroSecure, I believe."

"Yes, sir."

"And Angela? What became of her?"

"She died, sir... in the earthquakes...."

Seren takes on a more serious face. "The earthquakes, yes, it was tragic. And you are a captain, is that not so?"

"Yes, sir."

"So, captain, are you still attached to EuroSecure?"

"Sir, I'm now a captain with Search and Rescue. There is less call for fighter pilots. I accepted the new assignment because I am committed to saving lives."

Mark looks at him meaningfully.

Seren is not rattled. "Then, we are in the same business."

Mark grits his teeth but says nothing.

Seren looks distant for a moment. "I also seem to remember that Angela thought you and I looked somewhat alike, but I don't see it."

"Nor do I," responds Mark seriously.

"No, but apparently some others do. Tell me, why have you come to the tower today?"

"Search and Rescue found Ms. Vardeman unconscious several kilometers outside Rome. After we administered medical treatment, she spoke to us of her brother. Apparently the two had become separated."

Seren looks at his assistant, who confirms Mark's story. He asks, "What do we know? How can we be of service?"

The assistant comments, "My Lord, everything they are saying matches our records. But we do not know the whereabouts of the brother."

"Please extend to them every courtesy, and let's see if we can help them locate Ms. Vardeman's brother."

The assistant and everyone in the room, except Mark and Rakel, snap to attention. Seren turns to leave and as he does, he says to Mark, "Truly an honor to see you again, captain. Keep up the good work. A pleasure, Ms. Vardeman."

He bows his head slightly and proceeds out the door. The Sentinels quickly exit the room, following him. Finally, Mark and Rakel leave along with the original assistant.

He asks, "Should we find any more information, whom can we contact?"

Rakel replies, "I'm not sure. I'm in temporary quarters, and I have no technology."

Mark intervenes, "You can reach me through Search and Rescue. We're working on this as well."

The assistant smiles, "Please give our regards to your leadership at Search and Rescue. Lord Seren is eager to maintain good working relations with all such units of the Federation."

Mark and Rakel move toward the exit, somewhat relieved. As they do, Mark feels something stuck in his back.

"You're under arrest, Captain Knutson."

Not sure quite what to expect, Mark turns around and notices that, for the first time, Rakel seems a little rattled.

It's Massi.

Mark is surprised and relieved and a little angry. He wants to hit him, but he restrains himself.

"Massi, you freak! I ought to smack you."

"Knutson, you're such a punk. But hey, the buzz is that you had a private meeting with Lord Seren. What did he say? I hope you're reconsidering joining the Sentinels. You can't seriously want to be spending all your time just rescuing people. I know you. You're a player, a warrior at heart."

"My assignment will have to do for now. Excuse my bad manners, Massi, this is Ms. Rakel Vardeman, someone we rescued recently. Seren told his staff to help us locate her brother."

"Hmm, it looks like there are some definite benefits to Search and Rescue."

Rakel replies without smiling, "Charmed, I'm sure."

As they leave the tower, Rakel asks, "Who was that jerk?"

"Oh, that was Massi. Massimo Sansone. He's from Rome, studied in the U.S. but never graduated. I used to serve with him in the Praetorian Guard, well, actually a couple of stints. He's still in. He decided to transition into the new guard."

"He wants to serve and protect?"

"No, he just wants ascend up the food chain mostly."

"Not to change the subject, but let's change the subject. How do you think that went?"

"They let us leave alive, so I'm guessing that we didn't stir up any serious waves, except for that commotion in the Great Hall."

"Serenity Tower," Rakel scoffs. "Did you get that?"

Mark just keeps walking and does not reply.

They stop for a cool drink at a sidewalk café and sit, watching the people go by. After a short time, Mikhail, Tom, and John Wayne pass by and see them.

"Official business?" Tom jokes.

"Sort of. We just got back from the tower."

"How did that go?" John Wayne asks.

"We're still alive."

Mikhail asks, "Do you two have any more official plans?"

"Nothing official."

"Are you dating? ... Officially?"

Rakel responds quickly, "Yes, that's official!"

Mikhail laughs. "That's great. A great match-up!"

They part company, and Mark and Rakel go back to his apartment.

"How about a movie?" Mark asks.

"No, I'd like to go somewhere."

"A show?"

"Nope, none of the shows interest me."

"We could go to the beach later."

"Maybe later." Rakel mediates for a moment. "How about Paris?"

"Paris! But that would take... Uh, wait a minute. You know, I wonder if the topaz would take us there or maybe to Sweden."

"Topaz?"

"That's another one of the powers I have, to transport instantly to anywhere in the world. How about Sweden? I would love to see your home country."

"I made a promise not to return to Sweden until I find Erik and take him there. How about Paris?"

"Paris!"

"It's so romantic. And we could be back very quickly, if your stone works as you say."

"You know, Paris is full of memories for me. Actually, very happy memories."

"If it bothers you, we don't have to."

They hold hands, and Mark touches the stone. In an instant they are on the Left Bank.

"I guess my request was approved." Mark comments, somewhat pleased.

Rakel says, "Wow! I'd like to have a topaz." They are excited to be in Paris together. Mark takes her hand and they begin to stroll on the Left Bank.

But as Mark looks around, he is disturbed. No, this is not the Paris he once knew. There are no artists along the Seine, only greenery and fruit. There are crowds walking from place to place and intermingled he sees Sentinels, some in cloak. He begins to feel uneasy. As they continue walking, he looks around, trying to orient himself. And then he realizes. Notre-Dame has been leveled! How is that possible? Another terrible thought occurs to him. He ducks into an ally, pulling Rakel with him.

"We have to check something out."

In the twinkling of an eye, they are standing before the Eiffel Tower, or where the Eiffel Tower used to be.

The iconic, magnificent steel structure has been replaced by a statue in the likeness of Seren, about the same height as the original.

"I think I'm going to be sick. We need to get back home. He touches his topaz.

—20—

MORE THAN JUST A KISS

Mark and Rakel decide to spend Mark's day off by going hiking in the mountains and maybe to a beach in eastern Italy. Pinocchio packs them a lunch and dinner, and they mount aerobikes and head east, traveling until they find a suitable spot.

After leaving their bikes in cloak, they spent most of the morning hiking, laughing, and competing with each other. As he races against her, Mark is not accessing his stones. He's enjoying watching Rakel try to outrun him, to climb faster and higher than him, and to charm him. She's winning on every score.

They return to the aerobikes and sit in the shade to eat lunch. Rakel rests against a tree, and Mark leans against another tree opposite her. She has a far-off look in her eyes as they listen to Duke Ellington and his band play "Take the A Train."

"Mark, what you dream about?"

"You don't want to know."

"Probably not. Same here. These days, Mark, I have a lot of nightmares. I guess that's not surprising given everything that's happened in the last year. But those are only at night. I mean, what do you dream about for the future?"

"You seriously think there is a future?"

"I admit that things don't look good right now. We are fighting because we have hope. And it's not just the hope of heaven. We believe that because we are fighting, somehow, things will get better here and now, right here on planet Earth. Who knows? Maybe we can live normal lives one day. You are supposed to defeat Seren. That would make a huge difference. But what about the immediate future? Don't you have any dreams or desires?"

"A lot of those left with Dominique."

"I understand. I felt the same way after I lost my husband. We were team. We loved each other. We were good together."

Mark doesn't say anything. He just listens.

"I like you Mark. I like you a lot. You have those same feelings for me, I think?"

"Those kinds of feelings are dangerous. Whatever dreams we may have, whatever future we may have is probably going to be painfully short."

"*Carpe diem*, Mark."

"What?"

"We don't know how long we have. It may be short. If only we had world enough and time..."

Mark recognizes the line but doesn't remember who said it.

"Where's that from?"

Rakel explains, "Andrew Marvell, British, from a poem, 'To His Coy Mistress.'"

"How would a kickboxer know that?"

"I told you, I studied at Oxford."

Mark does know about *carpe diem*, seizing the day at hand.

Now Rakel is silent. They both just look around, enjoying the beautiful scenery. Mark, however, considers Rakel to be more beautiful than the scenery.

"Mark, I know you're a fighter, a warrior. We've talked about those special powers you have, that you can do things that are supernatural or superhuman. I'm dying to know what other powers you have. Where does such power come from?"

"Excuse me, is your name Delilah?" They both laugh.

Rakel responds, "No, not Delilah. In this case, we're working on the same side. I want to know precisely because we *are* on the same team. In fact, we are a team. We click. What's more, we have a lot of fun together. I could go on."

Mark smiles. Inside he still feels a certain conflict, maybe even guilt. He does like Rakel a lot, and he knows he's has even fallen in love with her. But can he give himself permission to do that? He again remembers what Dominique told him, the last thing.

He looks at Rakel. She needs him, and he needs her. The world that he loved with Dominique is gone. He doesn't know how much longer this world will last or what Seren's next move might be.

"Like I told you before, I am going to face off with Seren himself. You know or you've heard that Seren has incredible supernatural power. You haven't even seen the half of it. The only way to confront him, to defeat him, to kill him, is to come at him with a greater supernatural power and to know how to use it. Here's something you haven't seen before."

Mark opens his shirt and shows her the breastplate.

"They are beautiful! What are they?"

"Each of the stones represents a specific type of power. I'm slowly learning how to use each one. I assume that I will use them all on the day that I face Seren in combat. That moment is what I have lived for, until now."

"Face Seren in combat? What kind of combat?" Rakel seems a little shocked. "Could I possibly be a part of that?"

"Rakel, you are important to me, and your safety is important to me. I don't want to lose you like I lost Dominique. You have to stay out of this."

Rakel listens intently. Mark notices tears flowing down her cheeks. She makes no attempt to wipe them off.

Time to change the subject a bit.

"Let me demonstrate a few."

Mark walks over to a nearby tree about ten meters tall. He hugs it, grasping it firmly and rips it out of the ground by its roots. He then drops it, allowing it to fall and roll down the hill next to them.

Rakel is awestruck.

Mark clarifies, "It's not me; it's God. It's part of what I need to defeat ultimate evil."

"Sort of like the strength Samson had?"

"I guess." Mark then walks toward the base of a nearby cliff.

"Another stone gives me superhuman speed in running, and another somehow cancels the laws of physics."

At this, Mark jumps to the top of a nearby cliff, about fifty meters up. He then turns around and jumps back down, landing softly.

"Have you ever rescued someone like that? I mean, have you grabbed ahold of them and jumped with them?"

"Not specifically, I don't think."

"Would you like to do an experiment?"

Mark is a little leery, but it makes sense. If he had to rescue someone from a dangerous situation, it would have to work.

"Okay, it's worth a try." He puts his arms around Rakel from behind and supports her under her arms.

"Lock your hands together. I've got no seatbelt here! And bend your knees."

Mark bends his knees with her and leaps up. The two of them easily ascend to the top of the cliff.

Rakel is laughing. "Wow! That was exhilarating! I assume it will work going down as well?"

"I'm not sure. That sounds more risky."

Rakel laughs again, "Come on, Mark! You know that we both live to take risks."

Mark puts his arms under her arms, this time from the front. They don't make a move for a few intense moments. They've never been this close before and in such an intimate position. He looks into those lovely blue eyes and feels like he's falling already.

"Mark, I trust you with my life."

Mark jumps.

They both land softly and again start laughing. The laws of physics do not apply.

"Strength, speed, the ability to run like lightning. Is that all?"

"Oh, there are others. In time..."

After they talk some more, Mark and Rakel pack things up, get on their aerobikes, and head to the east coast. Mark knows a particularly beautiful beach with white sand that is blocked on three sides by towering high cliffs. Access to the beach by land is almost impossible so they are almost guaranteed to have complete privacy. When they arrive, they get set up in the large shadow created by one of the cliffs. The Mediterranean is crystal clear and blue, blue like the sky, blue like Rakel's eyes.

They sit and continue to talk, enjoying the view and each other. Eventually, the sun sets, and the moon comes out, rising over the eastern horizon. They almost don't notice. They are lost each other's company.

They take a stroll down the beach hand-in-hand. They are not talking now. Their hands are doing the talking.

"How about some music?" Rakel asks.

"Sure, you pick."

"How about some music to dance by?"

"As long as it's not tap-dancing."

Rakel laughs. "Even I can't tap-dance on the sand."

They continue to walk as her portapack plays slow music.

Mark turns to Rakel, and asks, "May I have this dance?"

"I thought you would never ask."

"Are things moving kind of fast here? I thought women liked to be chased for a while."

"But when a man saves a woman's life, well, that speeds things up a lot."

"Hmm."

He takes her in his arms and the two start dancing together very gently. They're both barefoot, so as they move, they shuffle the sand slightly. At first, they are gazing into each other's eyes. After a time, Mark holds her close. Yes, even closer still.

Suddenly Rakel pushes herself back from Mark. She looks at his chest, which is glowing.

"What is that?"

Mark opens his shirt. "It's the amethyst, the twelfth stone."

"What kind of power does it give you?"

"The power of love. It's the greatest of them all, according to Mikhail."

Rakel looks at it and looks at him and smiles. They continue dancing, and the violet-colored amethyst is glowing brightly.

As Mark looks at the moon, a thought occurs to him.

"I wonder," he whispers.

"You wonder what?" Rakel asks.

Mark separates himself from her and takes her hand. He looks at the moon which is large and has risen about halfway above the horizon. Its light is reflected in the sea in a long bright strip, a beam that ends at the shore's edge, at their feet.

"Hold my hand, and let's take a walk. Let's see if the laws of physics apply here."

They begin walking, and as they do, their feet are definitely getting wet, but they are not sinking. They look at each other smiling, almost giggling. They continue walking out across the sea.

"Does this make you nervous?" asks Mark.

"Why? Remember, I'm a risk taker. Are you nervous?"

"Yes, but not because I'm standing on the water. I'm nervous because..."

He turns and embraces her and looks deeply into her eyes.

"Is this a dream?" she asks.

"I sincerely hope not," Mark responds. He leans forward and kisses her, and she responds with passion.

"I love you, Rakel."

"*Jag älska du*, Mark."

Mark doesn't speak Swedish, but he understands. This is from her heart. They continue embracing and kissing.

After they're not sure how long, Mark pulls back and looks at her. "Rakel, will you marry—"

"Yes!!!" She interrupts him, almost shouting. Then she looks at him, smiling, "We have world enough and time."

Mark smiles back at her and responds, "I think that a kiss is a whole lot more than just a kiss."

They kiss again. The stars have come out and the moon is now full, just above the horizon. Mark and Rakel form a single dark silhouette against it, standing on the moonbeam and reflected in the sea. A violet light glows brightly between them.

And Dooley Wilson sings, "As Time Goes By."

PART III

—21—

THE STATUE SPEAKS

When they return late that night, Rome seems quiet. Mark makes sure Rakel gets home safely, but he feels sorry for anyone who would try to tangle with her. He returns to his apartment, happy. In fact, he realizes that he's been smiling most of the day and that his lips and cheeks are slightly sore.

Better get to bed, a big day tomorrow.

He lies down and falls asleep. At about four o'clock in the morning, he wakes up with a start. He sits up and looks around. Everything is the same, except that there is a mirror, a large one, in his entertainment area.

"Pinocchio, what is that? I don't see a reflection in it."

"I am not sure what it is, Geppetto. It has just appeared. It is not a standard mirror or a hologram, and I cannot see past the surface either."

Something is going on inside the mirror; he can't tell exactly what. *Okay, I'll bite.*

He gets up to investigate and walks toward the mirror. As he approaches it, he hears a distant voice calling his name. The voice seems familiar, but he's not sure who it might be.

Inside, there seems to be a lot of smoke, and he can't quite tell what's beyond the surface. He feels the stones on his breastplate and calls out his sword, helmet, and shield.

Let's do this thing, he thinks. He steps through the glass and into the world of the mirror.

Mark finds himself inside the Tower of Seren. The smoke has cleared away. And he sees Seren's statute standing in the middle, but no water is flowing from his hands. The Great Hall is vast, quite a bit larger than he remembered, and he doesn't see anyone there, and he doesn't hear anything.

Mark suddenly smells something foul. He looks around; the whole place seems to be empty. Then he hears a loud buzzing, which he recognizes. *The locusts are back.*

He prepares for combat. He looks up at the ceiling, and sees that they are in fact giant locusts and that they are beginning to swarm above him. He is about to raise his sword when he hears a voice calling out from behind him, "Mark!" He knows that voice; it's Rakel. He turns and runs back to her to reassure her.

"Mark, how did I get here? What are those things on the ceiling?" Rakel is never visibly frightened, but then she's never seen evil on this scale.

"Just stay behind me. I'll protect you."

Mark raises his sword and expects a powerful burst of light energy, but it doesn't happen.

Okay, I'll just take them on one by one.

A gigantic locust swoops down and lights in front of him. It is much larger than he is, and the sound of its whirring wings gets even louder. Then the locust jumps, only to be met by Mark, who quickly cuts off its head.

One down, Mark thinks. Then four more locusts land in a circle around them.

"Stay close," he shouts to Rakel.

Mark waits for the menacing bugs to make a move. When they do, they all attack simultaneously. He manages to slay two of them quickly, but the other two have snatched Rakel and are trying to fly away with her. She is struggling and fighting them. They are quickly joined by other locusts.

Mark, trying to keep his cool, studies the situation. *How best to save Rakel and kill them, without injuring her?*

He hears another sound behind him and turns. The gigantic statue of Seren has come alive and is standing with a drawn sword. Though it still seems to be made of stone, it is animated and moving. It then jumps off the platform onto the floor and moves toward Mark.

He turns back quickly and tries to kill several locusts, which he does, but the others have taken off with Rakel and have deposited her behind Seren's statue.

The statue speaks, "You want to save her, I'm sure! To do that, you'll have to go through me. You have seen my power in the past, but perhaps not recently."

The statue raises its sword and strikes the floor in front of it. "I will defeat you, and then I will make you watch my subjects sacrifice Rakel to me!"

It then rushes Mark, who meets it with sword and shield. Both their swords are on fire, and each time they strike each other, there is a thunderclap and a small explosion.

This is what Mark has trained for. He will prevail and rescue Rakel. He is not afraid of this thing, whatever it is.

Mark takes the offensive and actively engages the statue; it narrowly misses his attempts to strike. He then becomes more aggressive and moves ever faster.

But the statue reacts fast as well. *Time to take this thing up a few more notches.*

After it slashes at him, Mark jumps into the air to its left and strikes the back of its leg. The statue bellows, and Mark is gratified to see that it can feel pain. *Let's have some more of that kind of action*, Mark thinks.

He runs and jumps and slashes. The statue bellows again when Mark strikes its right hand.

Then the statue turns to the locusts and commands them, "Begin the sacrifice!"

It then swings back around and strikes the floor again with its sword. The bottom gives way and opens up into an abyss. Mark tries to leap up, but for some reason he is unable to reach Seren or Rakel.

He falls into the darkness below. Then he remembers that the laws of physics don't apply to him, so he breaks his fall with two power bursts from his hands, and he ascends, landing on the altar just in front of Rakel, his sword drawn.

"Now, Seren, you die" but the statue beats him to the punch and slashes his sword at him, cutting off his left arm.

Mark looks at the stump in disbelief and then looks at Rakel who is being prepared for sacrifice. She is tied to the altar.

"Mark," she looks directly at him and screams, "Wake up!!!"

Mark jerks awake. He looks around the room breathing heavily.

"Is there a problem, Geppetto?"

"You tell me!" Mark snaps back. "What happened to the mirror?"

"What mirror, Geppetto?"

Mark breathes a sigh of relief and begins to massage his eyes and his scalp.

Pinocchio announces, "Geppetto, you have an incoming call from a portapack. It is Rakel. Shall I allow her image to enter?"

"Yes!"

In seconds, a poor quality 2-D image of Rakel is standing before him, crying. "Mark, my love, are you okay?"

"I'm great, now that I've seen that you're okay! What's going on? Did you have a bad dream?"

"Not exactly, I just woke up with the most horrible feeling that you were in danger somehow."

"The only thing I need right now is a kiss from you."

"You want me to come over?"

"Get a cab. I'll meet you downstairs."

He stands up and kisses her faded image, and she kisses the air toward him.

It will take a few minutes so he lies down and decides to watch a slideshow to pass the time.

Rakel passes in front of him, wearing different outfits and sporting many different expressions. But he is weary of holograms. Virtual-reality. He wants the real thing.

After about ten minutes, the real thing arrives. Rakel buzzes him and ascends. She opens the door, and they rush toward each other, embracing and kissing.

Finally, they sit down on the couch and talk.

She asks, "What's going on?"

"I had a dream. A bad one. You and I were being attack by giant locusts, and Seren, I mean his statue, like in the Great Hall, drew his sword and came after us."

"Giant locusts?"

"Yeah, I've been seeing a lot of them recently."

"Really?"

"Well, in dreams and visions or something."

"What happened?"

"I was doing pretty well against Seren. I hit him in the back of his right leg and his right hand."

"Did he get any hits in on you?"

"Uh, well, sort of. I was doing well, but in the dream, you told me to wake up. And since I always do what you tell me, I did."

"Can I have that in writing or on a recording?"

The conversation dissolves into more kissing.

She whispers into his ear, "It won't be long now!"

—22—

DINNER IN THE METROPOLIS

"'Freder sees a monk in the pulpit, who preaches, 'Verily I say
unto you, the days spoken of in the Apocalypse are nigh.'"
Metropolis, 1927 silent film

Mark and Rakel have again planned dinner together in his
apartment. They hardly saw each other during the day's mission,
but they did find time to share their good news with their team
and other friends, all of whom were thrilled for them.

When she arrives and walks in the door, she drops the bag she
is carrying, and the two embrace and kiss and kiss, and they kiss,
and they kiss some more.

"I love you, Rakel, and I missed you today, I mean, the real you.
I forgot how to say 'I love you' in Swedish."

"*Jag älska du*, Mark!"

"Yeah, that."

Mark picks up the bags and puts them on his kitchen counter.

"So what's the surprise tonight? I was thinking maybe you
would cook a typical Swedish dish."

"Oh, didn't I tell you? I can't cook. I guess I never learned; I
studied kickboxing and tap-dancing instead. And then there was
the Special Forces training. And then... oh, never mind! Tonight I
brought spaghetti that I picked up at a takeout place. Hey, when in
Rome..."

"So are we eating at the table or on the floor again?"

"Everything tastes better and you're sitting on the floor
watching a movie!"

"Everything is just better when you're around."

As they are fixing their plates, a news update from the Tower of Seren appears. It's Santori, as usual.

"Friends and Romans, be assured that Rome is still the same, except that it's better than ever! The Bolla was beautiful, but it kept so many people out. Now, thanks to our Lord Seren, we've been able to extend the dream of the sweet life, the Roman peace, to so many more. Everyone is employed, and no one is hungry. The sick are healed."

Santori pauses for dramatic effect.

"And the good news of Rome's successes is spreading. The number of disciples is growing. Enthusiasm and hope for the future are almost uncontainable."

A projection appears beside him. It is a view of the inside of the Coliseum at the latest rally. He notes, "You see how much these 80,000 Romans love our Lord Seren."

Mark and Rakel stand there holding their plates, watching, and hoping this will be short. They see the crowds, the fervency, the shouting, the energy, the zeal, all this displayed before Seren, who stands waving at them all and smiling.

"Pinocchio, I guess there's still no way to shut this thing off?"

"Geppetto, as usual I have no control. But I think this is just a short preview of a longer presentation later this evening."

"Remind me to leave before that happens. I'm starting to lose my appetite."

Finally the transmission ceases. Mark and Rakel settle down with their spaghetti and begin their heart-to-heart.

"Mark, did you speak with Mikhail about arranging our upcoming big event?"

"I did. We're scheduled for Friday night, at the catacomb meeting place."

"I told Mei-Li, Iqhawe, and those I was working with and everyone else I could think of. They all seemed so happy for us!"

"And I invited Gabriel, Major Suravira, Tom, John Wayne, and the others I ran into."

"I assume Mikhail will help spread the word?"

"I think he will. We still have time to invite anyone we might have missed. After the wedding, he suggests we go for our honeymoon up north in the mountains. There's a safe spot there used by escapees that he recommends."

Rakel smiles. "I like the sound of that word, escapees. I only wish it could be permanent."

"It's not. But I'm counting down the days, the hours, and the minutes. I'm ready to seize the day!"

"I want to be yours, and I want you to be mine. I want our hearts to beat to the same rhythm and to have the same passions and to have a single purpose."

"I think most that's been pretty well spelled out for me. I just don't know what some of the details are, or exactly how you fit into it. I think Mikhail is going to explain more of that on Friday night. So you have other surprises? Which hundred year-old movie are we watching tonight?"

"I brought *Metropolis*. Do you know it? It's classic sci-fi."

"I know about it, and I know it's considered a classic. I just never took time to watch it. It's not a 'talkie,' and the special effects seem so primitive."

"That's why you have me in your life now. But first, I thought we could watch each other's holograms from past years. I brought a few holographic sequences from my personal library. I retrieved them while I was away. Even though they are from the early days of holograms, they're still pretty good. I assume you have some of yourself and your family?"

"Some, but I don't watch them much. I don't think they're very interesting. They're also a little primitive."

"I'm very interested, and I insist that you show me something, especially from your cowboy days! I've fed Pinocchio my files. Are you ready? Pinocchio, play number one!"

Mark settles back and watches as a large skating rink appears in reduced size in his entertainment center. In the middle, a beautiful blond skater is doing a routine. Her hair is in a ponytail, and she is very, very good.

"Zoom!" Mark commands.

Mark is impressed as he watches the young skater spin and do pirouettes. She whirls in circles on the ice, and she swirls in circles while in the air. It's a beautiful expression of the music accompanying her, much like ballet, perhaps even smoother. The skater is Rakel, possibly about ten years younger.

"So what do you think?"

"Nice legs," observes Mark.

Rakel hits him in the head with a pillow.

"You are so not funny! What you think of the style, the technique? I wasn't too bad, was I?"

"Why did you take up ice-skating?"

"I'm Swedish! It would be really weird if I did not I skate at all. People would say, 'You're Swedish, and you don't ice-skate? What's wrong with you?'"

"Okay, I get it."

"Do you ice skate? Or ski?"

"No, I'm from Oklahoma. I used to waterski some and roller-skate when I was younger. I don't think I could handle life up north with all the ice and snow."

Mark continues to watch Rakel skating, trying to focus on her technique and movements. Truly poetry in motion. She jumps in the air so easily.

Mark asks, "What's that move called? It's pretty impressive."

"That's a triple axel, one of the most difficult moves to make, or at least to do smoothly."

"And a lot of spinning. How do you keep from getting dizzy?"

"Practice and concentration."

"I also like your ponytail. You don't wear it much."

"No, I'm afraid not. My hair's not quite long enough currently. Sometimes I clip it back when I do kickboxing or tap-dancing routines, as you have no doubt noticed."

"With you, I don't miss much."

Rakel moves on, showing pictures of her family. In one series, it's just her parents and her at various stages.

"I am from Uppsala, just north of Stockholm. Here are some pictures of Erik and me."

They continue to look at pictures and primitive holograms from Rakel's life. Mark asks a few questions occasionally and finds it interesting, but all that Mark wants to know is sitting right beside him. She is an extraordinary woman in many ways, in quite different ways from Dominique.

Finally, Rakel sighs, "This is all very boring, I think it's now time for something from Oklahoma. I know about that musical, *Oklahoma*. I was never much into musicals, unless of course tap-dancing was involved."

"Pinocchio, access cowboy sequences."

A new scenario appears.

"A rodeo!" Rakel exclaims. "I always wanted to go to a rodeo. What did you do?"

"My dad was a roper, big rodeo cowboy, so naturally I followed him. He didn't teach me much about life, but he taught me a lot about roping and bull-riding."

Then, a much younger Mark bursts onto the scene mounted on his steed and spinning his lariat in the air in hot pursuit of a steer. He slings his rope and snags the steer on the first try. He then leaps from the horse, flips the steer, and ties up its legs."

Rakel exclaims, "I was a pretty good horseback rider, but I could never imagine roping a steer like that. Very impressive!"

"Not really. My time wasn't so good on that one. I did better in other attempts. You'll see."

They continue to watch Mark rope steers. Finally the bull riding sequences begin. Mark slides himself on top of the back of a bull. He holds on to what little he can, and the gate opens.

The bull spurts out in a wild frenzy, jumping in every direction possible, trying to eject its rider. Mark does fairly well for a time but eventually is thrown off. A rodeo clown runs into the arena, trying to distract the bull, and Mark escapes alive, once again.

"Explain to me what the point of that is."

"I guess is to show the bull who's in charge... And maybe a test of courage and manhood."

"It looks to me like the bull was in charge!" Rakel punches Mark's arm and begins laughing.

"It's not so easy! You should try it."

"I would love to! And you should try a triple axel..."

"Okay, touché."

They continue to watch rodeo sequences and a few scenes from Mark's family life. They view his family when they camped in the mountains and around lakes.

Mark exclaims, "Now *this* is boring."

"This was all in Oklahoma?"

"Yes."

"It's so beautiful."

Rakel becomes thoughtful.

"Mark, you have any video of Dominique? I don't mean to be rude or to pry. Perhaps it's too personal."

Mark says nothing for a moment. Finally he asks Pinocchio to play "The Prayer." At this, Dominique and her mother appear, sitting at their pianos. Rakel sits quietly.

It's difficult for Mark to watch, but it is also strangely encouraging to him. As mother and daughter play their pianos and as Dominique's mother sings, heaven invades the room.

Mark thinks to himself, *I guess her prayers were answered. I saved her life.*

When they finish, and the scene freezes, Rakel is wiping away tears. "No wonder you loved her so much. She was beautiful, and that piece was stunning. The whole thing was just beyond description."

Mark doesn't say anything. He looks at the floor for a time.

"Close program," he commands Pinocchio. Dominique and her mother and the pianos disappear.

""You need to talk?"

"No, not really. I guess I'm glad that you and she have finally met."

"I will not soon forget it."

Rakel reaches over and holds Mark in her arms. The two sit, silent, for a time.

Rakel finally gets up and takes her dishes into the kitchen area.

"Are you up for that sci-fi movie?"

"Sure. Let's do it, but remind me what this is about."

"Let's see, in 2027, wealthy industrialists have built a giant city, a metropolis, on the backs of laborers. The well-to-do live in their heavenly city while the workers sweat and suffer below. It's an old story."

"Metropolis? Why didn't they call Superman to help?"

"Hush, and listen. So the son of a wealthy man falls for this Maria woman, who is of the lower class and a sort of prophetess. She proclaims him to be the mediator between the two worlds. Anyway, enter a mad scientist who takes a robot and somehow turns it into the likeness of Maria, but this Maria, the false one, is a troublemaker. Oh, let's just watch it. You'll see."

They view *Metropolis*. About a third of the way through, Mark observes, "You know, for 1927, the special effects aren't that bad, better than I remembered. Pretty imaginative stuff, still not exactly like the 2027 I remember."

"Okay, but does anything you see remind you of Rome?"

"The city up top actually does have sort of megabuildings and bridgeways between them. Of course the aircraft flying around look like bi-planes, pretty primitive."

About two-thirds the way through, they laugh at the false Maria's seductive dance routine and the overstated reactions of dozens of men who are watching her."

Mark comments, "I guess in a silent film they had to exaggerate everything."

Rakel adds, "Yes, and especially the make-up. I think they're all wearing too much mascara, even the men."

Mark laughs until the false Maria mounts a seven-headed dragon.

Mark notes, "Well, now, that looks familiar."

"Really?"

"Yeah, I fought one of those in a hologame once."

"Let's all watch as the whole world goes to the devil."
False Maria, *Metropolis*

When it's over, Mark asks, "So they burned that robot at the stake, and the real Maria and Freder kiss and live happily ever after? All's well that ends well?"

"I guess. They have their mediator."

Mark quips, "But isn't a kiss just a kiss?"

Rakel hits him with the pillow again.

"And what about all that Tower of Babel stuff? What did you make of that?" Mark asks.

"Do you know of any towers like that around Rome?"

"Yeah, unfortunately."

Mark is pensive for a moment, and he goes on and shares some random thoughts.

"I guess I see maybe another similarity or two. The world up top was like a paradise, but there was kind of a dark world below, people suffering under the surface, sort of like the old Rome, the people outside the Bolla."

Mark thinks a little more.

"And I also thought about how Santori is trying to sell the new Rome as a paradise, but there is a dark, sinister world beneath the surface, almost like the lower class has been welcomed in, like lambs to the slaughter. Not really an improvement for the people."

"Nothing positive?"

"Yeah, there was Maria; I did like Maria."

"Which Maria, the real Maria or the robot Maria? Hey, maybe I'm a robot?"

Mark looks at her with a wry smile. "Maybe we both are."

Pinocchio chimes in, "Oh, that would be wonderful!"

Mark and Rakel both laugh.

—23—

WEDDING IN THE CRYPTS

"Thou hast ravished my heart, my sister, my spouse; thou hast ravished my heart with one of thine eyes, with thy one necklace."
Song of Solomon 4:9

The big day arrives. It's not an elaborate wedding; "just the fundamental things apply as time goes by." As Mark goes to the catacombs, he feels a little nervous, and he's not exactly sure why. It wasn't like this with Angela, and he never got to marry Dominique. Can this be real?

As he enters the room, he sees that everyone else has arrived early, except that he doesn't see Rakel. Mikhail approaches him and slaps him on the back.

"Are you ready, captain? This is an exciting day! One of the brothers has done a number of weddings and has agreed to perform the ceremony. And a sister plays the violin, and that will be the music."

"At least it's live." Mark notes.

"He looks around and sees John Wayne, Tom, Iqhawe, and Mei Li, along with others from his Search and Rescue team. *This is my family.*

Mei Li comes up to him and shakes his hand. She is smiling for the first time. "Congratulations, captain! I am very happy for you."

"Thank you," Mark is not sure what else to say, so he gives her a faint smile.

"But I still don't like you."

Mark stares at her for just a second, and then they both burst out laughing. Yes, this is definitely his family. That crack reminded him of his cousin Eva back in Oklahoma. That is exactly the kind of thing she would have said to him.

The violin music begins, *Canon in D* by Pachelbel; it's sweet and beautiful, approaching sublime. As Mark waits, he looks at the floor, remembers, meditates, and fidgets a little.

Finally, Rakel walks through the door opening. It occurs to him that he has never seen her in a dress before. Mark doesn't know where she got the one she is wearing, but it is beautiful, simple, and smart, much like she is. When she sees him, she bursts into a smile, and he does the same.

As Rakel approaches, Mark reaches out and takes her hand. Everyone in the room is smiling. They then all face the brother in charge of the ceremony.

"Dearly beloved, we are gathered here in the sight of God and these friends to join together in holy matrimony, Captain Mark Knutson and Rakel Vardeman.

"The bond and covenant of marriage was established by God in creation, and our Lord Jesus Christ endorsed this manner of life by His presence and first miracle at the wedding in Cana of Galilee where He turned water into wine. It signifies to us the mystery of the union between Christ and His Church, and Holy Scripture commends it to be honored among all people.

As the brother makes further remarks about marriage, Mark looks at Rakel with a certain awe. *This is not a dream*, he thinks. *Too bad. It's the best dream he's ever had.*

"Rakel, will you have this man to be your husband, to live together with him in the covenant of marriage? Will you love him, comfort him, honor and keep him, in sickness and in health; and, forsaking all others, be faithful unto him as long as you both shall live?"

Rakel smiles gently and answers earnestly, "I will."

"Mark, will you have this woman to be your wife, to live together with her in the covenant of marriage? Will you love her, comfort her, honor and keep her, in sickness and in health; and, forsaking all others, be faithful unto her as long as you both shall live?"

Mark answers, "I will."

"Mark, repeat after me."

"I, Mark, take you, Rakel, to be my wife, to have and to hold from this day forward, for better, for worse, for richer, for poorer, in sickness and in health, to love and to cherish, until we are parted by death. This is my solemn vow."

"Now, Rakel, repeat after me."

"I, Rakel, take you, Mark, to be my husband, to have and to hold form this day forward, for better, for worse, for richer, for poorer, in sickness and in health, to love and to cherish, until we are parted by death. This is my solemn vow."

The brother continues. "Bless, O Lord, these rings as a symbol of the vows by which this man and this woman have bound themselves to each other; through Jesus Christ our Lord."

Mark places his mother's wedding ring on the left ring-finger of the Rakel's hand, repeating:

"I give you this ring as a symbol of my love, and with all that I am, and all that I have, I honor you, in the Name of the Father, and of the Son, and of the Holy Spirit."

They both immediately notice that the ring is too small. Rakel smiles and puts it on her pinkie.

"Now, Rakel, are you ready with your ring?"

"Yes."

Rakel places the ring, which is actually rolled-up aluminum foil, on the left ring-finger of the Mark's hand, whispering, "It's all I could afford."

Then she repeats:

"I give you this ring as a symbol of my love, and with all that I am, and all that I have, I honor you, in the Name of the Father, and of the Son, and of the Holy Spirit."

Mark touches the tin foil ring, and before their eyes, it turns to pure gold. Rakel looks at him in wonder. She notices two faint lights in his chest through his shirt, one violet and the other green in color.

Then the brother joins the bride's left hand and the groom's right hand, saying:

"Now that Rakel and Mark have given themselves to each other by solemn vows, with the joining of hands and the giving and receiving of rings, I pronounce that they are husband and wife, in the name of the Father, and the Son, and the Holy Spirit. Those whom God has joined together, let no one put asunder!"

Everyone affirms, "Amen!"

Mark kisses his bride, and Rakel kisses her husband.

The violinist plays the processional, and everyone applauds as the happy couple walks back down the aisle together. The group has prepared some snacks for a simple reception, and the conversation afterward is animated.

Everyone lines up to congratulate the happy couple. It wasn't the wedding he had visualized. It was just the basics, even a little primitive and a bit unusual, being married among the dead. But this little cave had come to mean a great deal to him. It was the place he first saw a group gathered in hiding. It was the place where he returned and couldn't find Dominique but did find Rakel. *Ironic,* he thinks.

Rakel is smiling. It comes naturally for her. She knows just what to say to everyone, even to people she hardly knows. Neither smiling nor being conversation come naturally to Mark. He likes to watch her in action and in an odd way is proud to be with such an amazing woman. She needs him, and he needs her, like Dominique told him. Dominique was also amazing, but the two are so different in so many ways.

Finally, Mikhail comes up to the newlyweds holding an ornate box, trimmed in gold.

"I have a very special wedding present. Actually, it's a special present for the bride."

Rakel is very excited. "Can I open it now?"

"Oh, you must!" responds Mikhail. Mark is very interested to see what this gift is, but when she opens it, he knows exactly what it is.

"It's beautiful!" Rakel exclaims. She picks it up. "It's a necklace, isn't it? I've never seen one quite like it."

Mikhail answers, "It is a necklace. In fact, it's much more than just a necklace."

"I know what it is. Let me do the honors."

Mark takes it, holds it up and moves behind her. He fastens it around her neck.

"My love, it's time for you to become fully equipped as a warrior. The twelve stones on your necklace are the same as the twelve on my breastplate. I assume they have the same functions?"

Mikhail nods affirmatively and explains, "They are mostly the same, but of course your personalities and gifts will come into play. Mark, will you assume responsibility for her training?"

"I think I've just become responsible for everything about her, respecting her independence, of course."

Rakel looks at him intently, "Of course."

"Then, let's begin!"

Mikhail turns to the group and asks, "Has someone remembered to bring rice?"

At this, the couple is showered with rice and well wishes. Amid all the clapping and laughing, Mikhail leans forward and whispers to them, "Then it's time for you to learn what the topaz can do," and he touches the stone on Rakel's necklace, and Mark follows suit.

In the twinkling of an eye, Mikhail, Mark, and Rakel are transported to a high mountain top. They are surrounded by trees and are standing next to a cabin.

"I think I recognize this place." He looks at Mikhail, "Surely not. It can't be."

"Not to worry, captain. This is a gift for your honeymoon. You'll find everything you need here, food, shelter, and several changes of clothes. You're in no danger whatsoever, and no one will disturb you here until you are ready for training. It is actually Rakel's training, but you know the ropes, so to speak. And you are now both fully equipped. She only has to learn how to use the power of the stones. And of course you will continue to practice everything as a team."

Mikhail goes on with his instructions. "Up here, on the top of the mountain, you can relax and enjoy each other. It's down there in the dark valleys where you will find danger, temptation, trouble...and training. The only temptation on the mountaintop is that you might not want to leave...ever."

"How long should all this take?" Mark asks.

"Enjoy your honeymoon, and prepare yourselves. There is no night here, but back in Rome, the night is coming soon."

Mikhail disappears.

—24—

A GARDEN ENCLOSED

"Thy lips, O my spouse, drop *as* the honeycomb: honey and milk are under thy tongue; and the smell of thy garments *is* like the smell of Lebanon. A garden enclosed is my spouse; a spring shut up, a fountain sealed." – *Song of Solomon* 4:11-12

Mark and Rakel explore the cabin and the immediate surroundings. They conclude that they are in fact alone. They enjoy the breathtaking scenery, the mountain ranges, the trees, the lake below.

When they go back into the cabin, Mark looks deeply into her eyes, and says to her, "I love you, Rakel, with all my heart. I would lay down my life for you."

She responds, "The same for me."

"I guess impossible dreams can come true."

She smiles and strokes his face. "Mine has."

They begin kissing and embracing as they undress and lie down together. In innocent vulnerability, Mark gives his whole self and his whole heart to her, and Rakel willingly gives her whole heart and her whole self to him in love, trust, and complete intimacy. The two become one flesh.

They sleep for a time and when they wake up, they are pleasantly surprised to find the sun still shining, and a light breeze blowing in from outside.

"I'm starving!" exclaims Rakel as she jumps out of bed. "What's to eat around here?"

She rifles through the cabinets and the refrigerator and is delighted to find a wide variety of foods, particularly several types of fruit. She picks up an apple, turns to Mark and asks, "Do you want a bite? I hear it's really good!"

"Now that has to be the oldest line in the history of the world, don't you think?"

"Yes, I believe it is." They both laugh.

They eat other things and later decide to go out for a walk. In spite of Mikhail's reassurance, Mark is still a little nervous. He doesn't want to lose her like he lost Dominique. He occasionally feels his breastplate and checks Rakel's necklace. He just wants to make sure everything is working and in order.

Mark reaches over and touches the amethyst on her necklace and it emits a violet light. The amethyst on his breastplate also lights up and is visible even through his shirt.

"Which one is that?"

"The amethyst unleashes the power of love, my love, remember?" They embrace and kiss again.

Rakel suddenly pushes him back and asks, "Hey, I wonder if I could uproot a tree."

"Activate the jasper, the first stone. Just touch it!"

Rakel complies and runs excitedly to a tree about three times her height, hugging it and ripping it out by its roots.

Mark yells to her, "Hey, just be careful how enthusiastically you hug me!" They both laugh.

"Now, I think you're ready for the sword, the shield, and the other armor. Touch the second two stones. The blue sapphire is the sword, and the baby-blue chalcedony is the shield, helmet, and the other gear." Again, she complies and her armor and weapon appear. She admires the sword.

"This sword is amazing! Beautiful. I love the inset stones."

"And very powerful. As you learn to use it, you will see it glow and strike out like lightning against your opponent."

Mark takes withdraws his sword. "Cross your sword with mine," he tells her. As she does, the two blades produce the starburst of light, even greater than Mark remembered.

Rakel comments, "I knew we make a great team!"

Mark observes, "I think that the power is even greater when the swords of two warriors touch. It's not just doubled. It seems like it went off the scale.

Rakel is experimenting with her equipment. She touches the same stones again, and they retract.

"Now touch the striped brown sardonyx; that will give you speed. I'll race you down to the bottom of the valley."

She agrees, and they both take off running down the slope and are laughing as they go. They reach the valley's bottom in a matter of seconds.

Rakel stops and sits down on a tree stump. She continues laughing. "This is really fun, so when do we get down to some serious business?"

"Some serious business appears to be headed our way. Not to worry, I've taken on this character before. I have total confidence that you can, too."

Rakel turns and looks. "I don't see anything."

Mark replies, "Oh, sorry, touch the emerald. That's the oracle stone. It allows you to see into the invisible world. People in cloak with technology, and supernatural beings that no one else can see unless they have this equipment."

She touches the stone and looks up. She sees a demon dragon approaching.

"If I'm not mistaken, that is Apollyon, or some version of him. I met him early in my training. You have your weapon and armor, your shield and helmet. You might need to activate the jacinth, the eleventh stone; that will give you healing if you need it. You'd better get ready, because I think he is."

As with Mark, Apollyon begins flapping his wings and rises into the air slightly. He hurls two flaming darts at them, which they easily deflect with their shields.

Mark then commands, "Shield up!" They both raise their shields immediately. This move protects them from the hail of fiery darts thrown by the devil. Neither is wounded.

"Go ahead and take it out," Mark says to Rakel.

"I'm interested to see how long it is between its attacks."

"Not long."

Rakel waits and times each pause. Finally, when she has fended off one shower of fiery darts, she jumps up and runs toward the demon like lightning. When it sees her approaching, it makes ready to launch more darts, but it is too late. Rakel jumps, spins in the air with her sword extended, and decapitates the monster.

Mark runs toward her, "Awesome job! What do you call that move?"

Rakel smiles, "I would call that a triple axel."

"Sweet."

Rakel asks, "Okay, what about the other stones? I can't remember which ones do what. How do you remember?"

"Once you've activated them and use them, they come on automatically, depending on the needs you have at the time. Some seem to work in response to thought impulse. You've used the stones that give you the sword and armor, strength, speed, the transporter, and love. With me, you experienced the sardius, which exempts you from the laws of physics. You've also seen the power of transformation in the chrysoprase. And of course, there is love."

"That's my favorite!"

"The remaining stones are the fourth, the emerald, the oracle stone, which allows you to see into the invisible world, like with oracle glasses, except a lot more. The beryl makes *you* invisible, but not necessarily to demons, which are also imperceptible to the rest of the world. Again, number eleven is the jacinth, which permits you to heal yourself and others."

"Let's try the invisible thing." She touches the stone and vanishes. Suddenly Mark feels a hand whacking him in the butt.

"Hey!" He taps his emerald, and can see where she is. "I'm going to have to pay attention around you!"

"You'd better stay sharp, Mister!"

"Okay, I've been warned!"

They both become visible again, and Rakel continues to ask more questions.

"What's the one that enables you to emit a power burst from your hands? I want to try that."

"That's the seventh, chrysolite."

Mark turns and hurls a power burst against nearby trees, all of which fall flat to the ground.

"Wow, awesome! With that power you could take out a lot of opponents."

Rakel turns to a different group of trees and tries to do the same. Nothing happens. She touches the stone several times, but still nothing.

"What's wrong?" she asks.

"Maybe nothing's wrong. Look at your boots."

Rakel looks down and sees that her boots have been turned into solid gold, but it is a gold that is flexible and that seems radiant with power.

Mark asks, "I'm wondering how a kickboxer might put those boots to use?"

"Let's find out." Rakel runs toward another group of trees, jumps in the air, and stomp-kicks the closest one. A power burst comes from her boots and topples about fifteen trees.

"Whoa! I can definitely put this to good use."

Mark and Rakel continue working on honing her skills with the new weapons and powers. They practice as a team.

"Let's duel with our swords," Rakel suggests.

"Hey, this is not fencing. Someone could get hurt."

Rakel withdraws her sword, "Like you, perhaps?"

"Okay, but promise to be gentle."

"That's not going to happen!" She attacks him boldly, and he meets her every move defensively.

He asks, "But what if you hurt me?"

"That's not going to happen either. You're too good. I have confidence in you."

They continue to spar until they are tired. They return to the cabin and lie down together. Violet light is shining strong.

Later, they talk about what is ahead.

"Do you think we're ready to go back?" Mark asks.

"I never want to leave this place."

"That's the temptation. We need to go back. We have to think about the mission."

"Then I'm ready to go back. I never want to leave your side. I want to be there with you and for you."

"Same here."

"So what do you think the mission is exactly?" Rakel asks. "It looks like we're both going to confront Seren, but how?"

"Every time I ask Mikhail questions like that, he always has the same answer, 'In time you will understand.'"

—25—

DOUBLE-CROSS

Mark and Rakel finally decide to go back to Rome and back to reality. They gather up their things and transport to their apartment.

Rakel studies her new home and remarks, "There's definitely some work to do here."

"Anything you want to do, my love. But I wonder how much time we will have to spend here."

They watch several official news reports and are disturbed by what they see. The atmosphere in Rome has changed. There seems to be a growing fanaticism, a greater outpouring of love for Seren, almost resembling worship. They watch massive rallies at the Coliseum and the Circus Maximus in which Santori is stepping up the rhetoric for Seren and against rebellion of any kind. The gatherings are packed with enthusiastic believers; some seem almost frenzied in their adoration.

Santori begins with reports of progress, a wide array of healings, even some people raised from the dead. He explains, "The powers of our Lord Seren are growing, and his disciples are slowly learning. We are now better able to share knowledge of this power with more countries and peoples, especially with those who have aligned themselves with Rome."

He goes on to an overview of economic prosperity, jobs, housing, and food for all. He admits, "It is obvious that we are succeeding where the Roman Senate failed. I confess that I was a part of the Senate for years. In our meetings, I openly expressed my reservations about change; it's a matter of public record. Of course I did not know about Lord Seren until later. I'm excited that all our dreams and hopes are finally coming true! One could say we are creating heaven on earth. And it seems that nothing is impossible for us."

Santori then feigns a troubled expression, "In spite of these great, encouraging reports, I'm very sad to have to tell you about a tragic problem. It is only one problem, and a very big one. In fact, it is the same problem that Rome has long had in her history. Of course, the New Rome is free and open to all. Lord Seren welcomes visitors and immigrants to share in the sweet life, the good life. I'm sure you have noticed even greater increases in security and in the presence of the Praetorian Guard and the Sentinels. This is because we are concerned about one very real threat: Christianity."

The crowd begins booing.

"I'm sure we all know of the history of this violent sect. Do I need to mention to Crusades or the millions who have been killed in the name of the Nazarene? I think not. Sadly, we have become aware of underground activity of Christians right here in Rome. We have been diligent, but they are insidious, cunning, and evil. They will stop at nothing to destroy this paradise that our Lord Seren has made possible. Help us to identify groups or individuals that you suspect may be affiliated with this rebellious and dangerous movement."

Mark and Rakel are surprised but not surprised. Mark observes, "It was only a matter of time."

"Do we need to continue watching this?" asks Rakel

"I think we need to catch up and be aware of what's going on." Mark replies.

Santori continues his update, emphasizing the progress and sharing glowing reports, one after another. Finally a holographic projection shows Seren in the Coliseum. The arena is packed with admirers, adorers, worshipers. As he speaks, it is sometimes hard to make out what he is saying, because the outcry is so great. All are pouring out love for Seren, some fall on their faces before him, some sing and raise their hands. All seem to be worshiping. Mark notices that some are cutting themselves and crying out.

"I've had enough of this," Mark scoffs. "Let's go out somewhere."

Almost as soon as they are ready to leave, Mark receives an emergency i-call from Tom, who seems agitated.

"Captain, please come! Sentinels and PGs have surrounded one of our meeting places, a house on the outskirts. Stand by. I'll send you the coordinates."

Once they receive them, Mark and Rakel transport themselves to the scene and remain invisible. They have the advantage that the Sentinels cannot see them, and they can also see the Sentinels who believe themselves to be invisible.

About thirty of PGs and Sentinels have in fact surrounded a house and are moving in. Within seconds, three giant megabots lumber down the streets toward the location.

Mark communicates with Tom. "They are ready to take action. We will intervene."

But before they can do anything, one of the megabots fires at the house and demolishes it. Another fires on the PGs and Sentinels, and the third picks off those the second one missed.

Mark and Rakel just look at each other, confused. Then, two of the megabots fire on the third and destroy it. The remaining two quickly leave the scene.

"This doesn't even make any sense," says Mark. "Let's go check for survivors. The Sentinels and PGs have all become visible. They are either dead or almost dead.

Mark scans the house for survivors and doesn't see any life signs. He raises Tom on the i-com. "What just happened? Are the people in the house dead? Can you tell?"

Tom replies, "A report I picked up on was that the house contained about thirty Christians. But I'm not certain now. I'm not sure who those people were or even if anyone was inside. When I learned about the raid, I sent them a warning. Maybe they all got out. And now it seems that the megabots have taken out Seren's own troops. It's strange."

Rakel calls out to Mark, "Over here!"

Mark joins her and sees a severely wounded Praetorian Guard lying on the ground. He turns him over carefully. When Mark sees who it is, he becomes visible.

"Massi!"

Massi looks up at him. "Knutson! What are you doing here? What happened?"

"Two of those megabots took out your squad."

Massi looks dazed and squints his eyes, "Whaaa...?"

"Close your eyes, Massi. I'm here to help."

Mark activates the healing stone, and Massi is completely restored in an instant.

Massi sits up, still not completely coherent.

"Massi, you've been double-crossed. Things aren't what they seem here in Rome."

Massi sits up and looks around. He mutters, "I think those Christians did something here, and I'm going to get to the bottom of it."

"It wasn't the Christians, Massi! You've been betrayed by Seren himself."

Mark and Rakel disappear.

"Knutson!" Massi cries out. "What the hell is going on? Where are you?"

He then looks at his hands and feet, his arms and legs, and massages them. He gets up and quickly leaves the area.

The next day, Santori appears in their apartment with a long face. Mark speculates, "Maybe this will be the official version."

Santori begins, "I regret to inform you, citizens of Rome, that last night, on the outskirts of Rome, the members of the Christian sect massacred fifty people and destroyed one of our megabots."

Santori displays a hologram showing the house in ruins and the bodies of Sentinels, PGs, and other people who were not there last night.

Santori explains, "As you can see many of our security forces heroically gave their lives to defend the innocent."

"Tom, what's going on? Are those new bodies real?"

"I'm afraid they are this time. I don't know what they're up to. I can assure you that it is not good."

The same night, Mark and the team have a meeting to discuss the problem. Why is this happening?

Mikhail stands up and addresses the group.

"The church is growing because many Romans and visitors have become disillusioned with Seren. As they say, 'all that glitters is not gold.' We are increasing in numbers also because some have read the Scriptures; others knew someone who was a believer before the earthquakes. Those witnesses have gone on to the City, but their testimonies remain with us, and we have been profoundly affected by them."

"Because we are growing and because Rome is also growing, the problem is becoming worse. Fierce persecution is coming, and with the increasing numbers, we are having a harder time covertly evacuating believers and others to safety. Inevitably, in this atmosphere, some of our people will be caught.

"We have no doubt that the security forces are sending spies to root out the problem. Their plan is to infiltrate groups, to pretend to be Christians, and to gather intelligence. This will become worse before it gets better.

"The situation is very grave. In fact, we know that three of our cells were hit last night and that many believers were taken prisoner. Others were killed on the spot. The chatter that Tom picked up on was some kind of ruse or diversion."

Everyone is upset. Mikhail warns them, "Stay calm, stay prayerful, and keep your eyes on the One. My guess is that they will announce details on a forthcoming update."

Mark speaks up, "Mikhail, Rakel and I were there last night! We watched the whole thing go down. We were prepared to take on the guards and protect the Christians. But the truth is that we did nothing! We just sat and watched megabots take each other out and slaughter the security force that was there."

Tom adds, "I can confirm that there were thirty believers in that house. They are all dead."

Mikhail clarifies, "They have all gone to the City where they will be forever safe. Our immediate concern is for those taken prisoner. They will suffer before they depart."

Mark asks, "So what's the plan? Are we going to rescue them?"

"We will not."

Mark scoffs, "That doesn't make any sense. We can, and we should."

Many mutter in agreement. Mikhail speaks up, "My friends, we all have a purpose. These things must happen. Seren will grow in power, and things will get worse before they get better. This time of tribulation was foreseen by the prophets thousands of years ago. It is all part of the end. And each of you has a part, a mission. We need to pray and to focus on our mission."

After the meeting, Mark says to Mikhail, "I don't get it."

Mikhail responds, "I understand. Stay focused. Your time is approaching soon."

"And is it Rakel's time?"

"Your time. Your team. I meant both of you. Stay strong."

—26—

THE SEVENTH SEAL

The next day, Santori appears in Mark and Rakel's apartment, as usual, but this time he is speaking from the Coliseum. He's addressing a full house, a noisy, animated audience.

"Friends, Romans, countrymen, we have good news! Because of the diligence of our security forces, we rounded up the perpetrators of last night's massacre."

At this, about forty people are led onto the field. They appear to be about a dozen or more families, husbands and wives, some youth, and small children. As they move along, they are met with cheers for Seren and jeers for them. Many of the spectators throw trash at them or anything that's available. They are all dressed in white robes that look like bed sheets.

Santori exclaims, "I give you Christians, the enemies of Rome, the adversaries of our Lord Seren! Today we will be seeing what happens to those who would attempt to destroy our paradise. May these serve as an example."

The guards quickly exit the stadium floor and leave the group huddled together in the center. Within a few moments, six hungry lions are released through open gates, and the crowd thunders its approval. The holographic figures projected into the apartment are small, but Mark and Rakel can see the terror on their faces. One of the group seems to say something, and they all gather together, kneel, and bow their heads.

Mark is burning with anger. He looks at Rakel and asks. "Are you ready to go?"

Before they can depart, Mikhail appears in the room. Mark says to him, "I hope you're going with us this time!"

"I'm not going, and neither are you."

"What!? We can't just stand here!"

"We can, and we will." Mark tries to activate his transport stone, but it does not work.

The lions circle the group, and eventually strike, roaring and bellowing. The carnage is horrific. Within just a few minutes, bodies and body parts are strewn everywhere. And the lions are feasting on the corpses of their prey. The crowd is going wild, yelling, and giving a thumbs-down sign.

Santori once again addresses the enthusiastic audience, "So shall it be with all enemies of Rome and of our Lord Seren. But, fellow citizens, the show is not over. There is more!"

Mark is visibly even angrier. "I don't understand. We could stop that. We have the power."

"Your hour is soon to come. Both of you will confront Seren. But this group is now forever safe with the One in the Celestial City. Keep your eyes focused on your mission, the assignment for which you have trained so diligently."

Rakel asks, "But how? When?"

"At the right time, you will know," Mikhail responds calmly.

Rakel says, "I'm not sure I want to watch anymore of this."

"You need to. Be strong. You need to watch."

Now, workers are carrying large crosses onto the field, about fifty of them. They then space them out and drill large holes into which the bases will be sunk. The crowd is again booing, hissing, and yelling obscenities. Mark and Rakel can feel the hatred even through the hologram.

Santori cries out, dramatically, "Bring out the criminals!"

Sentinels bring out the prisoners in chains. Santori exclaims, "These Christians have killed the innocent! They have killed our Sentinels and our Praetorian Guard members. These oppose our Lord Seren. We have prepared for them a very fitting execution. Begin!"

At this command, the prisoners are lined up, each next to a cross, and each is then thrown down on it. Workers pound large nails into their wrists and their ankles.

Rakel begins crying, and so does Mark. Mikhail insists, "Please, watch just a little longer."

Mark sees something that makes him uneasy. He puts his arm around Rakel. "Pinocchio, try to match any of the figures in this hologram with holograms in the library."

Rakel wipes away tears and looks at Mark; then she looks at the hologram.

"One match," Pinocchio announces.

"Oh, God, Mark! Tell me it's not..."

Mark commands, "Blow it up to life-size."

Pinocchio complies, and they watch with horror as workers nail Erik, Rakel's brother, to a cross before their eyes. They elevate him and the cross, life-size, right in their living room.

Rakel buries her head in Mark's chest, crying almost uncontrollably. "I can't watch anymore. Can we go somewhere else?"

Mark commands Pinocchio, "Reduce the image back to original size."

As the scene continues, all the prisoners are finally nailed to the beams, and the crosses are sunk into the ground. The crowd is feverish with excitement, a bizarre combination of happiness and hate. The prisoners cry out to God in pain.

Mark shouts out, too, "Mikhail, we could stop this! God could stop this!"

After a few more minutes of suffering, the captives are all drenched with some kind of liquid. Then, the workers ignite the liquid, and the crucified become human torches. Shouts of praise for Seren are heard everywhere.

"It's time to transport," Mikhail announces. He takes their hands, and they are instantly translated to the Roman countryside, beneath a tall, majestic tree.

Mikhail assures Rakel, "Your brother is also now with the One in the Celestial City."

181

But Mark is still angry. "I don't understand. We transported here. We could have transported there! We could've stopped it. Erik didn't have to die."

Mikhail responds, "Take time to get some rest, both of you. Rakel, you need time to grieve and mourn. You will find comfort. And by the way, your number is coming up. You're next at the Coliseum. Your hour has arrived. You need to be thinking about a plan, about exactly how you will confront and engage Seren. I believe you will see that plan very soon."

After resting and grieving for a time in the country, Mark and Rakel return to their apartment.

"Tell me about Erik. I'm sure you have many happy memories."

Rakel calls up pictures, videos, and holograms and makes remarks on each one.

"I wish I could've known him," Mark comments.

"He always had such a good attitude, unlike his sister. He made me laugh a lot. He had such a good heart. After the explosion and his injuries, we were both desperate to find help. Erik had always taken things in stride, but his injuries left him very depressed, and he stayed that way for years, bitter at God. I heard about what was going on in Rome, and I thought, what do we have to lose? Then, shortly after we arrived, we became separated. That's apparently when I was taken prisoner."

"Evidently he became a believer. We will see him in the City. That's what Mikhail says."

"You know, it occurs to me, that he didn't go anywhere much after his injuries. He stayed at home, watching movies."

"What kind?"

"Oh, a little bit of everything. I remember there was one movie that really spoke to him, Ingmar Bergman's *The Seventh Seal.* Do you know it?"

"I've heard of it. I may have even watched parts, but it was in Swedish, and I found it kind of boring."

"Pinocchio," Rakel asks, "can you show it?"

"Only in 2-D and black-and-white. It has English subtitles. Apparently it has never been upgraded.

Mark asks, "Bergman. That name keeps coming up. Did it have Ingrid Bergman in it also?"

"No! It was a film by Ingmar Bergman, the great Swedish director. Would you still like to watch it, even though the beautiful Ingrid Bergman is not in it?"

"Why should I care? I have the beautiful Rakel sitting right here beside me."

"Perhaps it will help you to understand Erik's anguish."

A Christian knight and his squire return from the crusades. The Black Plague is sweeping through their land. As they approach their home, Death appears before the knight and informs him that his time has come.

The knight challenges Death to a chess game; if the knight wins, he will go on living. The Knight and Death play the game over the course of the film as people die all around them. For the knight, the game is a ruse, an attempt to distract Death until he can do, in his words, just "one more good thing."

After the film is over, they sit quietly for several minutes.

"That was depressing! What the heck was that about anyway? What did it all mean? I confess that I'm a little lost."

"The silence of God," Rakel explains. "It says in Revelation that after the Seventh Seal was opened, there was silence in heaven for about a half an hour. Anyway, that's what Erik thought, that God was unexplainably silent, that God did not care about him or about what had happened to him."

"Obviously his attitude toward God eventually changed. So what about that chess game that the hero was playing with Death? He said that it allowed him time so that he could do one more good thing. He lost, and a lot of people died anyway."

They continue discussing the film. And after a while Mark becomes pensive. "It *was* a depressing movie, but it gives me an idea...."

Mark thinks for a moment.

"Pinocchio, call up the chess game." A board and chess holograms appears in the entertainment section.

Rakel looks it over. "I see what you're thinking. You want to engage him in the game of war and strategy."

"Do you play chess?"

"Never. Never have. It always seemed so boring. You know me. I like fast action. I'm not one to sit around and think a lot. You'll have to give me a quick tutorial."

"Well, I figure we will challenge and battle Seren in the Coliseum, on his turf, in his theater, for all the world to see. And what better way, since we have all these powers at our disposal? He has powers, too. He has his own strategies. I think he would be intrigued by the idea."

"Show me how it works."

"Pinocchio, start a game run by the system."

The pieces are holograms about one meter high and very life-like. The pawns are foot-soldiers, and one of them moves first. The opponent's pawn matches the first move.

A knight on his horse leaps over the pawns in front of him and takes his position.

"You see? Pawns are limited and slow. They can be effective in good strategy, even crucial in the end game. It's best to hit them from a distance or from behind."

"And how do the knights move? Do they always jump?"

"Not necessarily. Knights are strategic because they move forward two spaces and to either side only one space. They attack at angles."

As the game progresses, the bishops enter into the growing web, the battlefield where no pieces have died but in which a slaughter is imminent. Mark continues to explain the game to Rakel.

"Basic chess strategy is to effectively use the varying powers of all your pieces. Game-winning moves often involve combinations of pieces."

"Watch. I think check-mate is coming up."

The white queen is distant, observing the black king. Regicide is afoot. The white knight advances slowly and methodically. Black players are capturing white players, but the white players are willing to make the sacrifice. The black players become overconfident.

Just when the black side is about to declare victory, the knight jumps to queen's level 6. Placing the king in check-mate. The knight is protected by the queen, though she is distant, her power is felt. The king cannot move. His people cannot protect him or slay the knight.

The black king must die.

—27—

WHITE KNIGHT, WHITE QUEEN

Mark calls a meeting of his team in his apartment. John Wayne, Tom, and Mikhail show up. For a time they watch goings-on in the Coliseum. The rallies continue, and so do gladiatorial contests, and the execution of Christians.

During all the festivities, Seren's high priests are making sacrifices to him, human sacrifices. Six altars have been built before his holographic statue. About every fifteen minutes, six human hearts are cut out. Seren is not present, only his hologram. Santori's hologram continues to lead the worship celebration.

As the team watches, Mark observes, "I think something's changed. Those people who are being sacrificed are doing so voluntarily. They actually seem happy. It must be some kind of honor. Why would anyone do that?"

Mikhail answers, "Because they believe he can raise them from the dead. He has promised great rewards to those who make that ultimate sacrifice."

"But can he deliver?"

John Wayne interjects, "I've seen him raise some people from the dead. At least I think they were dead."

"Captain, do you have a plan? I believe that the hour is now," says Mikhail. He adds, "You know that I cannot be a part, and this time, not even to save your lives."

"I hope you're not chickening out," quips Mark.

Mikhail responds, "Oh, no! I've taken on Seren before and have beaten him. To this specific battle only you and Rakel have been called. And your team, of course. What else do you need?"

"We intend to engage Seren in a sort of chess game. For that, we will need to appear to be more than just gladiators. Can the transformation stone make us appear to be a medieval queen and her knight?"

"It can, but it will only be an appearance. You have specific images of these two in your minds?"

"We do."

"You will still need to use your shields for protection. Remember, Seren plays with fire. You might get burned."

"That's a risk we'll have to take. We'll also need the support of two well-placed Praetorian Guard members for some muscle and some major electronic interference. We'll also need two white horses,."

John Wayne responds, "Then you have come to the right people!" They continue to discuss the plan in more detail.

As they conclude, Mikhail adds, "As for the horses, those I can provide. At our rendezvous point outside Rome?"

"That should work."

After the team leaves, Mark and Rakel talk for a while.

"Are you sure you want to do this?"

"After seeing Erik suffer and watching what Seren did to him and to those others, nothing can stop me. Are you having doubts now?"

"I know how you feel, but no, no doubts. This is all new to me, and I'm not certain how this is all going to play out."

They transport to the arranged meeting point where Mikhail is awaiting them with two white horses, which have been saddled and are ready to ride. They check each of their stones and ride the horses around the countryside for a short time until they feel like they're both ready.

Mikhail sends them on their way, "I will not be there, but the One will, and His power will give you success. Have confidence in that."

Mark and Rakel touch their transporter stones and are in the Coliseum instantly, although invisible for the moment. Though they are on the stadium floor, no one can see them. What seem to be priests are overseeing sacrifices at the altars, and the crowds are worshiping Seren's image and praising him.

Mark and Rakel touch their transformation stones. Suddenly they appear in full view of all spectators in the Coliseum. Their appearance has changed; they are now the White Queen and the White Knight; both are wearing white capes and are mounted on white horses. On Rakel's head sits an ornately jeweled, golden crown. Mark's shiny steel helmet and armor glisten in the sunlight. Their horses are restless, as if ready to do battle. A hush falls over the crowd.

Mark hears Tom and John Wayne chattering on the i-com.

"I make two snipers, occupying sniper boxes four and six. I can disable their weapons without their knowing it. I'll keep an eye out for any other possible threats."

Santori's hologram stands and quiets the crowd. He addresses Mark and Rakel, and his voice is amplified. Ear chips facilitate Universal Translator so that everyone can hear the conversation in their own language.

"It seems we have special visitors today! We welcome you. What are your names and where are you from?"

As Mark replies, his voice is also amplified for all to hear, "As you can see, the White Queen and her White Knight. We have come to play chess with the Devil."

The crowd roars with laughter, and Santori laughs as well. He then becomes very serious.

"But, Sir Knight, we all know that there is no Devil. However, we would enjoy seeing a contest. What would you like to face first? Wild beasts?"

Rakel responds, "We would prefer to play chess with Death, but for now, bring on your wild beasts. And make your preparations for a chess game tomorrow at this same time."

Santori gives the signal, and six gates are opened. From each, a hungry lion emerges. The crowd applauds and then quiets down quickly, as if eager to see what will happen next.

Mark and Rakel make no moves. The hungry, ferocious felines charge out onto the stadium floor and begin pacing.

The White queen and the White knight dismount. The White queen removes her cape to reveal her armor. The crowd is intensely interested; many lean forward, no doubt eager to see blood, any kind of blood.

The White Knight calms the horses, holds their reins, and stays with them. As the White Queen goes out to engage the lions, she produces her sword but does not use her shield. Three of the lions charge her, and as they do, she extends her sword, jumps, and spins, creating the effect of a buzz saw. In so doing, she quickly slays the first three.

For the moment, the crowd is quiet, apparently eager to see how she will handle the other three. These likewise begin their charge, but this time, she leaps and strikes one with her right boot. The big cat flies into the air about ten meters back, dead. She then turns, lands, and jumps, stomping one and sweeping the other in the head, crushing their skulls.

Santori stands up and applauds. "Sir Knight, your queen is most impressive! After we remove the bodies of her defeated foes, how may we serve *you*?

"Do you have any lions left?"

Santori gives the signal, the gates open, and six more lions appear. Rakel stays with the horses this time, and Mark runs forward quickly to meet his would-be predators.

As the lions circle him, Mark remembers trying to run from lions in the Parco Centrale. Now the stones have given him special abilities that technology did not.

He races over to the closest lion and tears him apart with his bare hands. At a nearly blinding speed, he then rips up the other five, one after another.

The audience sits in stunned silence, but eventually, they all applaud. Mark returns to Rakel and comments with a certain sarcasm, "I think they like us."

Everyone in the Coliseum is giving a thumbs-up to the White Knight and the White Queen. Santori likewise stands up, and his hologram also gives a thumbs-up.

He says, "It seems you have found favor with the people of Rome. We therefore honor you today as mighty warriors."

Mark shouts to him and to the crowd, "We will return tomorrow to play chess. The stadium floor is the board. Please make appropriate preparations. Be sure all your strategic pieces are in place and ready to do battle."

"Understood," Santori answers.

They remount their horses and vanish.

—28—

THE CHESS GAME BEGINS

The White Queen and the White Knight return to the Coliseum the following day. Santori is there.

"It's him, not his hologram," Tom assures them. "Looks like they consider this pretty important."

When they appear, the crowd bursts into a thundering applause.

Santori stands and addresses them, "You are most welcome, but we still do not know your names. May we therefore address you as 'My Lady' and 'Sir Knight?'"

Mark calls out, "You may. And you have prepared a chess game for us, I hope?"

"We have," answers Santori.

Eight gates open around the base of the stadium, and eight robots appear. Mark recognizes them. They are used regularly in the games and are programmed for gladiatorial combat. Sometimes they have a human holographic image on them and appear human, but not this time.

Mark is not sure what powers these pawns have. *And they don't know what powers we have either.*

The shiny, metallic robots step forward, their swords drawn. Mark and Rakel vanish along with their horses. The robots struggle to find them and scan feverishly.

Mark and Rakel suddenly re-appear without their horses behind two of them. Mark slashes down on the head of the one in front of him, and it falls to the ground, smashed into pieces. Rakel jumps and kicks the other robot from behind, shattering its torso.

A second group of two gladiator-robots steps forward with swords and maces. Mark and Rakel stay visible. The robots swing their maces and their swords alternately. But this time Mark and Rakel simply extend their swords, which emit a burst of energy, frying the robots and all their circuitry. The two fall over backwards, spitting sparks. The crowd applauds wildly, eager to see more innovative displays of fireworks and superpowers.

The remaining four robots attack more aggressively. Of course, they feel no desire for revenge over their fallen comrades. They're just robots, doing with they're programmed to do.

Mark whispers instructions into Rakel's ear. They both transform into robots that are identical to those approaching them. The crowd loves it, and all applaud. The noise level is almost deafening.

Robots don't become confused, and they don't spare feelings, so they attack. In the confusion, they strike at each other. Mark and Rakel join in the fun, and each destroys one of the robots, and watch while the remaining two fight and eventually destroy each other.

Mark and Rakel quickly transform back into the White Queen and the White Knight.

As soon as the field is cleared, the floor begins to shift and open, as often occurs in the Coliseum when the entertainment scene is undergoing a major change. Once the operation is completed, two large castle battlements rise up from the opening and begin to move forward. The ground closes behind them.

Mark and Rakel wait for their first move, which comes in the form of old-fashioned cannon fire. Every time a cannonball comes toward them, they vanish and appear elsewhere. The stadium is filled with smoke and smells of gunpowder.

The castles move deliberately but are not fast. Mark and Rakel continue the vanishing maneuver until they finally decide to attack the rooks and their defenders. They leave their horses and approach on foot. Large black pots appear on top, and the defenders begin pouring hot oil down the sides. Mark and Rakel avoid being burned by moving at a faster speed. The crowd has a hard time keeping track of them.

Next, large rocks are catapulted from the battlements. Mark and Rakel fend them off or disintegrate them with starbursts form their swords.

Finally, Mark leaps up on top of one of the castles and discharges a power burst, and Rakel jumps up on top of the other and stomp kicks the defenders. They leap from the towers to the floor and return to their horses, remounting them.

Mark then addresses Santori, "Yes, this is all very ingenious, but I hope you brought in stiffer competition for us today."

Santori replies, "I believe that we have."

After just a few moments, two gates open at the other end of the field, and two knights emerge with scarlet armor and lances. Mark and Rakel vanish and re-appear with their horses, which they have remounted.

"This should be interesting. Two gladiators against two medieval knights in full armor." Rakel says to Mark.

He quips, "Forget the gladiator thing. I'll be the cowboy, and you be the kickboxer."

Santori calls to them, "We do have complimentary lances for you, should you need them."

Mark replies with a not so subtle scorn, "No, thank you, we never learned how to use lances."

The two knights begin their charge, lances forward, from the other end of the Coliseum floor. Mark and Rakel also charge. Rakel surges forward at the oncoming knight, prodding her horse to a full gallop. The crowd is almost out of control with anticipation.

As she gets close to the knight on her side, Rakel grabs hold of the saddle horn, steers her horse to a sudden movement to the left, and jumps up with her boots on the saddle. She then leaps high in the air, and when she comes down, she stomps him in the chest. The blow sends him flying off his steed, about fifteen meters away from it.

The knight's horse comes to a quick stop. Rakel lands easily on the floor, goes over to the defeated knight, who is unable to get up. She draws her sword. The crowd applauds enthusiastically.

Meanwhile, Mark is charging directly at the other knight, drawing ever closer to him. He has taken off his belt and transformed it into a lariat, which he spins over his head.

As he approaches, he nudges his horse to the right and tosses the lariat, which falls and loops down around the knight's waist. Mark spins the rope around the horn of his saddle, and pulls it tight. The knight pops off the horse with a jerk and falls to the ground. Mark dismounts, and goes to the knight, speedily using the remainder of the lariat to tie up his hands and feet. He then pulls out his sword.

With blades drawn, Mark and Rakel look to Santori and the crowd, who have been shouting and cheering enthusiastically for the White Knight and the White Queen. They all vote a thumbs-down. Mark and Rakel sheath their swords in defiance.

Mark shouts out, "I hope you have some kind of real challenge for us today."

Santori stands and addresses them, "Sir Knight, you and your queen are full of surprises. Perhaps we may have a few surprises for you yet today."

Workers come and assist the fallen knights off the field. As two new gates open, Mark turns to Rakel and whispers, "I'm sure these will be the bishops, but I'm not sure exactly what to expect here."

In fact, two dark figures wearing what look like ecclesiastical robes emerge from the gates. The crowd is silent. Everyone wants to know what's next.

As they approach, the two dark figures brandish their blades, but their hoods are still covering their faces.

Tom comes on the i-com, "Mark, Rakel, they're scanning your minds. Be careful what you think! I'm not sure your armor will protect you from it."

Mark moves to the right, and Rakel walks to the left, hoping to separate the two. Mark approaches his opponent.

"En garde," he says. When the mysterious figure removes its hood, Mark is stunned. It's Angela, or what appears to be Angela.

"Marco! I am so happy to see you! I hope you have forgiven me for leaving you."

Mark is momentarily speechless. *This must be an illusion, but it's so real. How could they possibly know those details?* His mind tries to process the reality of the situation. He knows that he has to focus and disbelieve what he is seeing.

Meanwhile, Rakel confronts the other dark figure. It removes its cloak and hood.

It's Erik! He drops his sword and extends his arms toward her. "Rakel! *Jag älskar du*!"

"Erik!" She cries.

Mark shouts, "Rakel, it's not Erik! They are not real. They're accessing our minds somehow."

Mark engages the false Angela in a sword fight. *This thing, whatever it is, is very good.* It seems to know his next move every time. *Better act on impulse, without thinking too much. It's worked before.*

He then charges Angela erratically, and he eventually stabs her in the heart. As she falls, she is transformed. She cries out in pain, and then she becomes a giant, wounded locust. Mark cuts off its head and turns looking for Rakel.

But Rakel was only distracted for a second. She has delivered a deathblow to the false Erik, who quickly changes into another dying locust and falls to the ground. She cuts off its head.

Santori stands and addresses the crowd. "I think all gathered here will agree that this has been a most entertaining performance! We salute you, and we give you a thumbs-up."

The crowd stands to its feet and roars its approval. Everyone without exception gives them a thumbs-up.

When they settle down, and the noise level decreases, Mark addresses Santori. "And where is your master, Seren?"

"Our Lord Seren has many responsibilities, as you no doubt know." Santori looks up at the hologram of Seren. "But I am sure he is watching this contest somehow. He is taken a great interest in the White Queen and the White Knight."

Mark replies, "I hope he is watching right now. I'm issuing a formal challenge to a duel, right here on the Coliseum floor. The White Knight and the White Queen against him and his queen, if he has one."

197

Mark draws his sword and grasps the handle with both hands pointing it downward. With considerable force, he plants it in the ground down to the hilt. The golden bejeweled handle sparkles, and everyone who sees it wants it.

"We'll be back tomorrow at this same time. You may inform your Lord Seren that tomorrow he will meet his end in this place."

Mark and Rakel remount their horses, and the two vanish.

Workers and Sentinels and even some spectators rush to the floor of the Coliseum. One at a time, they try to extract the sword from the ground, but no one can. Even the strongest among them ends up frustrated.

Santori commands "Leave it there, I'm sure our Lord Seren will be able to pull it up tomorrow. I'm also certain that he will use that very sword to slay the White Queen and the White Knight."

At this suggestion, the crowd roars with applause and shouting. They continue praising Seren, and more people line up at the altars to present themselves as sacrifices.

KNIGHT TO QUEEN'S LEVEL 6

On the following day, the White Knight and the White Queen appear on the floor of the Coliseum. Seren, not his hologram, is on his elevated platform, waiting for them. Before him are six bloody altars and a line of people, eagerly waiting to be sacrificed.

Seren speaks, "Citizens of Rome, the White Knight and the White Queen do us a great honor by appearing before us in our humble theater."

Seren claps, and the rest of the crowd applauds with him. The Coliseum is packed full, and the event is being broadcast in all the nations of Europe and in many other parts of the world.

Mark and Rakel dismount, and Mark walks over to the sword handle and easily pulls it from the ground.

"Sir Knight," says Seren. "You are impatient. I could have spared you the trouble."

"It was no trouble at all. Do you have no queen?" Mark asks.

"I have no need for a queen, not as yet."

"That's a pity. You would find a queen a strong ally."

"Rome is my queen!" Seren retorts as he raises his hands, motioning toward the crowd.

Seren then becomes serious and raises only his left hand. Mark looks at Rakel, shouting, "Shields up!!!"

They both drop to the ground under their shields. Fire begins to rain down from the sky and covers them. They do not move until it ceases. When it does, they both look up over the top of their shields.

Seren is on his platform, and he leaps from it and lands on the stadium floor not far from them. He is cloaked in a scarlet cape, from which he produces a long sword.

"Captain Knutson, we meet again. Yes, I can see through your disguises. You are not as innocent as you have previously appeared. I know you have been given a number of powers. I'm just not certain which ones. But you can be sure of this, I also have special abilities, many of which you know nothing about."

"What we have is more than enough to beat you," answers Mark defiantly.

"And you, my dear, Rakel. We did find your brother, Erik. And we made sure to move him to a more stable location. Permanently."

Rakel is not rattled. She says nothing.

Seren draws his sword. "Why don't we start simply? I would like to test your skills."

The audience is riveted. The three begin almost playful exchanges. Clashes and clanks resound all over the Coliseum. Mark strikes, and Seren blocks. Seren pulls out another sword to block Rakel's advances. Then Seren strikes, and Mark blocks. They all three move in irregular circles, testing each other. Seren is studying them, and they are studying Seren.

After a few moments, they move faster. The crowd is watching breathlessly, but the movements are soon hard to follow. At one point, Seren clips Rakel's left leg above her boot, which gushes blood. Seren laughs.

"Don't let your guard down, my dear. A pity you don't have better armor."

She touches the wound, and it heals instantly.

Seren observes, "So you have that power? What a waste. That is no power at all. Before this is over, you will see my power. In fact, you will join the others at the sacrificial altars. And you will willingly give your lives for me."

Mark engages Seren even more aggressively, but they don't seem to be making any progress. At this rate, the swordplay could last for hours. Something needs to change.

As he thinks this, he strikes Seren's sword, and the two are locked together as they continue to circle each other. When they break apart, everyone looks at them, amazed.

Seren has transformed himself into Mark. And the two continue to battle each other. One of the Marks yells at Rakel, "Strike him down, now!" It's definitely Mark's voice.

Both Rakel and the crowd are confused. All eyes are moving back and forth between two identical White Knights. Rakel then transforms herself into Seren, and Mark follows suit.

Finally, Seren changes back into Seren. And the three circle each other so fast that it's almost a blur. Once again, the perplexed crowd doesn't know quite who to cheer for.

At length, all three become Mark, and then all three are Seren again, and they alternate identities at will.

Mark shouts out, "Rakel! Touch the oracle stone."

As she does and Mark does the same, they can see which one of them is Seren. Once Seren realizes this, he returns to his original form. Mark raises his right hand and emits a power burst."

Seren laughs sarcastically, "Am I a dog that you come at me with sticks?"

Seren then begins to hurl flaming darts at them in an almost continuous barrage, and they must drop and stay close behind their shields.

Seren fires his darts, and they respond with power bursts from their swords. It all becomes a dazzling fire-and-light show. The audience is enraptured. But nothing seems to be working; neither side appears to be winning.

Seren stops for a moment and taunts them, "Surely the White Knight and the White Queen have not exhausted their powers! You're unable to beat me. Look at me! I am alone and unharmed, and there are two of you."

"I guess were going to have to turn up the heat," Mark responds.

"You want to turn up the heat?" Seren asks. "I think that's an excellent idea!"

At this, Seren raises his left hand to the sky and is immediately transformed into a scarlet, seven-headed dragon at least four stories high. Mark and Rakel put up their shields to protect themselves against multiple torrents of fire. They slowly back away from the dragon to re-group.

The audience, on seeing his latest transformation, begins worshiping Seren even more. They cry out, "Seren is Lord. Seren is God. Seren cannot be defeated."

Rakel calls to Mark on the secure i-com, "What's the plan?"

"A combination move, the most effective in chess. Distract him. That may give me an opening."

"But which head do I try to strike?"

"Touch your oracle stone, repeatedly if necessary. I'll signal you when I think the time is right."

As she does, she can see that the third head from the right is the vulnerable spot.

Rakel asks Mark, "Do you see it?"

"Yes! I'll move directly toward it."

"Roger. I'll go to the left side and strike him over there."

"No way to do this without getting burned."

"That's a price we're going to have to pay."

They both advance slowly, holding their shields in front of them. So far their armor has held. Then, they separate and come at the beast from two different directions. They hear Seren's voice roaring and laughing.

"Fools! You think your pathetic weapons can defeat me!"

Mark shouts, "Now!!!"

At this, Mark and Rakel leap into the air. Seren expects that they will both strike at the heads. Rakel is on the left side. The three heads on that side take aim and discharge an incinerating blaze.

Rakel leaps through a wall of flames but drops short without slashing at the heads and lands at the dragon's rear claws. Though severely burned, she strikes its leg with a decisive blow, slicing off some of the scales. She then crumples to the ground.

The wounded monster bellows, and the center head bends down to locate her. In the meantime, Mark has leapt into the air with his sword raised, passing through a wall of flames. Though severely burned, he brings the blade down with full force on the vulnerable spot on the third skull. The beast thunders again and cries out a shrill cry.

The serpent slowly starts to shrink and eventually collapses back down to the size and appearance of a man. Mark drops in front of him, his sword extended forward.

Seren is stunned. He is staggering from the wound in his right leg. He feels his head and then looks at his bloody hand. He looks at Rakel and then at Mark.

Mark, pointing his sword toward Seren, shouts at him, "Checkmate, you son-of-a-bitch!!!"

And Seren reels and falls to the ground, apparently dead. Mark heals his wounds and runs over to Rakel, who has collapsed, and heals her burns.

Tom calls Mark on the i-com, "You two had better get out of there, now! I have closed all the exits except for the south gate. Move out, now!!!"

Mark and Rakel jump on their horses and gallop toward the south gate, which is not far from them. The stones don't seem to be working. Mark feels his chest and realizes that he has no stones at all. They have lost their shields and armor and longer look like the White Knight and the White Queen.

For only a few short moments, the crowd is stunned in disbelief, quiet. They are expecting that Seren will heal himself somehow and get up. When they see that he is not moving and is still bleeding and in fact appears to be dead, their anger erupts.

Hordes of them pour down the stairs and the sides of the arena, and Sentinels move in, but they are not firing.

As Mark and Rakel charge through the gate, it closes behind them. Tom informs Mark, "I've misdirected the other Sentinels and PGs, and they're looking for you over at the north gate. It may buy you a little time."

Within just a few moments after they emerge from the giant amphitheater, John Wayne arrives on an aerobike with a second one in tow.

He dismounts and yells at them, "Get off the horses and get on these! And make tracks fast!"

They mount the bikes and take off while John Wayne and Tom continue to misdirect traffic.

In the Coliseum, there is shock, anger, and weeping. All security forces in Rome and surrounding areas are placed on a state of high alert.

—30—

ESCAPE FROM BABYLON

"Whoever holds the devil, let him hold him well;
he will hardly be caught a second time."
Johann Wolfgang von Goethe, *Faust*, Part I

Mark and Rakel look like themselves again, completely unable to hide their identities. Several who saw them leave the Coliseum area raised their cameras to capture their images.

They race across Rome, heading for the rendezvous point. They hope to escape detection but know that is nearly impossible. Everywhere they look, they see their holograms popping up, informing the citizens of Rome that the two are wanted, hunted, and hated.

They increase to a high rate of speed. Rakel looks in back of them and shouts to Mark.

"We've picked up a tail, in fact, three."

Mark glances back several times and reaches down to the side of his aerobike. There he finds a small blaster. He glances at Rakel, but he sees that she doesn't have one.

The pursuing aerobikes open fire. Mark and Rakel take evasive maneuvers. Mark knows they can't outrun the aerobikes, so they'll just have to outwit their drivers. He signals Rakel on i-com just before he makes turns, ascends or dives.

Within only a few seconds, yet another vehicle is chasing them, a Black Raven XP-3.

Tom's voice comes over i-com.

"Mark, they have orders not to kill you, only to capture you both. But if I were you, I wouldn't allow myself to be captured."

"Roger that."

Mark ducks into tight spaces and weaves his way in and out of buildings large and small. Rakel mirrors Mark successfully, but the two pursuing aerobikes do not. They vanish.

"I think we've lost them."

"Think again," Rakel yells.

The Black Raven has found them and is opening fire. Mark sees that they are blasting very carefully. They are trying to disable the bikes, so he continues to use evasive tactics. He is trying to avoid the plasma bursts, which are striking ever closer. He and Rakel weave in and out of buildings, dive under bridges, and shoot through parks.

After a short time, Mark thinks they have lost the Black Raven. But Rakel yells to him, "We have the three aerobikes again!"

Finally two of the bursts from the pursuing aerobikes find their mark. Once they hit and disable the fleeing bikes, Mark and Rakel descend slowly and finally land on a cushion of air. They dismount quickly and run and quickly find themselves trapped, surrounded by buildings and walls, with no exit.

When Mark pulls out his side arm, a plasma burst knocks it out of his hand, scorching his skin severely. Finally, both he and Rakel raise their hands in surrender. The three PGs dismount and walk toward them.

Without warning, one of the PGs fires on the other two; they fall to the ground. He takes off his helmet.

Mark is shocked. "Massi!"

"Knutson, I don't know what the hell is going on in Rome. I think Seren and his people have double-crossed us. I'm going to need time to try to figure all this out. But I owe you one. Take these two bikes and get out of here!"

"Massi, how are you going to explain it to those two?" Mark looks at the two PGs lying on the ground.

"They'll wake up in a few minutes." Massi tosses him his tranquilizer gun and a PG access card. "Here's the evidence. Take it with you."

"Massi, I..."

"Shoot me, and get out! Remember, this is your last free pass from me! Shoot me now!"

Mark hesitates but finally does so. Massi falls to the ground.

They mount up and take off quickly.

When they reach the rendezvous point, a Search and Rescue ladybug craft is there to receive them into its belly. Mark does not know the pilot. They take off in cloak and proceed first east to exit Italian airspace, and head north on a course going around Seren's domains.

The pilot explains, "They told me to take you to the destination of your choice. I guess that way it will be a total secret. You know the airwaves are hot with news about what happened and assurances that the two perpetrators will be caught, tortured, and sacrificed to Seren or, I guess, to his memory."

Rakel asks, "How about Norway? I know a lot of good places to hide there. And at least for the present, Norway is outside Seren's sphere of influence. I have friends there."

The pilot responds, "Yeah, but you should be careful just the same. You need to see what's in the media right now."

He switches on a holographic projection of a news report. They see Seren's body being removed from the Coliseum, having been placed on a stretcher. There is Santori, crying, giving passionate assurances that the murderers will be brought to justice. They see mourners everywhere wailing and weeping.

Santori assures the people of Rome that Seren's disciples will continue to build a new Rome for a new age. But he also declares a time of national mourning throughout Seren's domains.

Mark puts his arm around Rakel. They can finally relax.

"It's done. It's what I trained for. It's what we trained for."

Rakel reflects, "I think about those German officers who tried to assassinate Hitler and failed. You know, in Sweden, we have not forgotten the Nazis and their evil."

"Wasn't Sweden neutral?" Mark asks.

"Yes and no. We did permit German troops to move through our country, but we also supplied the Allies with critical intelligence. And Sweden was a safe haven for escaping Jews and other conscientious objectors."

"My kind of place," Mark comments.

"My parents taught me about that time in history and passed on stories they heard from their parents and their grandparents. They warned me about it from the time I was a child. They always said that it could happen again. Different name, different faces, but the same sick vision. Maybe that's why I joined the Scandinavian Special Forces unit in intelligence."

Mark sighs and puts his feet up. "I'll have to thank Mikhail, Iqhawe, and Mei-Li when see them again for the training we received. It's gratifying to know that we have rid the world of yet another wicked tyrant. Except we succeeded where those German officers failed in their attempt."

"That must have been horrible for them, to have risked so much, only to see Hitler alive again after the bomb blast."

When they arrive in Norway, they are put up in a small house used by Scandinavian Security. In many ways it resembles the cabin where they spent their honeymoon, except that it has technology and some weapons.

Mark wonders, "The weapons are fine, but will we ever get the stones back?"

Rakel responds, "I suppose they were only for battling Seren. Whatever the case, we got the job done."

"Maybe it's time to start the honeymoon or to fulfill it in an even greater way?"

"Maybe the honeymoon should never end," Rakel responds.

They spend two glorious days in the mountains, almost carefree. They maintain regular communication with Tom, who has sent them an enhanced security surveillance program and regular updates about what measures are being taken to find them. Rakel is also in touch with friends and former co-workers from Scandinavian Security, who have promised additional support if needed. They feel safe and confident in their hideaway.

"Have you seen or heard from Mikhail?"

"No, not a word. I guess he has other things to do."

"I remember he said that he wasn't going to be involved in the fight. I guess that Adam and Eve had to strike back alone."

Rakel wrinkles her brow, "I hadn't thought of that, but there might be something to it. Anyway, I feel avenged for what they did to Erik. For what Seren did to all those poor people."

"And I feel that for Angela. I was pretty angry at her. But nobody deserves to die like she did."

Mark adds, "I wonder what's happening down there. We haven't had Santori appearing uninvited in our living room with updates, not that I miss them. At least here we have the option not to watch."

Rakel turns on the system. "Let's see."

The headline story is Seren's funeral. He is lying in state in the Tower of Seren, in the place where his statue used to stand.

"Now, he's a *real* statue," Mark jokes sarcastically.

They watch the seemingly endless line of mourners passing by, each struggling to catch a glimpse of the corpse. They hear the funeral dirges, the wailing, and the weeping. The commentator is not Santori.

He narrates, "It is a time of unbelievable anguish and uncertainty. We have lost our great leader, and many have lost hope. The people of Rome are confused and discouraged. Seren's disciples have tried to reassure everyone that they can maintain the level of life that we all enjoyed under Seren's leadership, but many wonder if life can ever be the same. Some sources—"

An outburst of sudden shouts interrupts the commentator. And the crowds of mourners fall silent. Someone near the body cries out, "His hand moved! I saw his left hand move!"

The crowd is stirred, and all eyes are fixed on Seren's left hand.

Mark and Rakel both stand up. Mark cries out loudly, "What the...?"

Rakel responds, "No, that can't happen!!!"

As they say this, both Seren's left and right hands begin to move. Everyone in the Great Hall is in shock and disbelief. And Mark and Rakel share those feelings.

Seren's chest begins rising and falling. He is breathing again.

Rakel asks, "Is this one of your nightmares? Tell me this is not happening!"

Seren slowly raises up on his left elbow and looks around. He then bends his knees and as he does, excitement spreads throughout the Great Hall. Several disciples rush toward him and slash their wrists and crying out. The crowd shout his name repeatedly and quickly begin chanting it.

"Seren! Seren! Seren! Seren!"

Finally Seren smiles, and he stands up. The world is watching, and the world is riveted to what he will say.

Seren proclaims, "I am back! Life, the power of life, has conquered death. I alone have conquered the grave! Cancel the funeral. Let the celebration begin!"

The multitude in the Great Hall falls on their faces and worship him.

"Follow me, and you will never die! Eat the fruit of my trees, live in the prosperity of my empire. You will never be sick again. Together we will create heaven on earth."

Both Mark and Rakel fall back into their chairs, in a state of shock. They raise Tom on the i-com.

"Tom, tell me that was faked!"

Tom pauses a moment and responds, "I'm afraid not. I'm afraid it was for real. I guess I'm just afraid..."

—To be continued—

Made in the USA
Charleston, SC
14 July 2016